The Test

A Novel

Nathan Leamon

CONSTABLE

CONSTABLE

First published in Great Britain in 2018 by Constable

1 3 5 7 9 10 8 6 4 2

A CIP catalogue record for this book is available from the British Library.

ISBN: 978-1-47212-954-3 (hardback)

Typeset in Bembo by SX Composing DTP, Rayleigh, Essex
Printed and bound in Great Britain by Clays Ltd, Elcograf S.p.A.

Papers used by Constable are from well-managed forests
and other responsible sources.

Constable
An imprint of
Little, Brown Book Group
Carmelite House
50 Victoria Embankment
London EC4Y 0DZ

An Hachette UK Company
www.hachette.co.uk

www.littlebrown.co.uk

THE TEST

For Ness

PROLOGUE

'I don't consider myself a pessimist. I think of a pessimist as someone who is waiting for it to rain. And I feel soaked to the skin.'

Leonard Cohen

Friday 2.15 p.m.

Australia	348 all out (119 overs)
England	20 for 2 (6.3 overs)

He plays.

He misses.

My heart stops.

From my angle, you can't tell a miss from an edge. So for the beat after the ball passes the bat, my heart waits. Waits for the keeper and slips to erupt.

They don't.

Heads and hands go up as one, the keeper skips sideways, the crowd gasps. But no appeal follows, just the collective in-breath of a play and miss. My heart starts to beat again.

I glance up at the screen and watch the replay. The ball has jagged sharply away from the bat. Too good. Too good for anyone.

If the fast bowler gets it right, the ball hits the ground four metres from you, ricochets off the turf at over 30 metres per second, and thuds into you or your bat one-eighth of a second later. If the ball deviates on pitching, you don't have time to react. If it moves enough, you will miss it, regardless of how good you are. If it moves the wrong amount you will nick it, and that's your day over.

3

I'm sitting on the balcony, trying not to fidget. I'm trying to not adjust my pads, to not fiddle with my bat handle, to not get up and pace the dressing-room floor. The effort of just sitting still is wearing me out.

I look back up at the TV, and now the cameras have cut to me, leaning back in my chair, feet up on the balcony rail in front of me. Thankfully, I look more relaxed than I feel.

There are good watchers and bad watchers. At the best of times I am in the latter category, and we are in a real hole here: well over 300 runs behind, and two wickets down already. The clouds have rolled in, and the new ball is snaking around venomously on a pitch that looked bland and unthreatening an hour ago when we were bowling on it.

I was getting showered and changed when the wickets fell, so I ask Grub, our wicketkeeper, to fill me in on what I've missed. There are coaches around, good ones, but they sometimes watch differently. Pay a man to watch a lion and he will do it. Tell a man he is about to go into the cage with the lion, and he will watch it in a very different way.

'The left-armer's going mainly across us. Nothing's shaped back in that I've seen. Good gas, mind.' The tension has thickened his Geordie accent.

'Right-armer's gone away mostly, mixing in his wobble-seam. They've bowled well like; need to see these two off. Get through this next half-hour.'

I nod.

Easier said than done at the moment.

Tuesday morning

'Mac, congratulations on your appointment. How does it feel to captain England?'

It still sounds odd, ridiculous in fact, to my ear.

'Look ... it's a very exciting opportunity. The series is beautifully poised and, obviously, to walk out at Lord's in charge of England for the decider in an Ashes series will be a great moment. It's a boyhood dream.'

'Is this a long-held ambition? And would you like the role to become permanent?'

'Rob is the England captain. I'm just keeping his seat warm until he's well again.'

'Your personal form has been poor of late. Do you think that will have a negative effect on your ability to lead the team?'

The questions keep coming, probing, needling. I'm letting as many go as I can, and trying to dead-bat the rest. This is not just about cricket at the moment. The series has arrived at the sort of climax that attracts attention outside of the usual fans and journalists. We are, briefly, on the front of the newspapers rather than the back. So the room is packed, and for every familiar face in front of me, there are another couple I don't know.

'The Australians have been critical of England's tactics so far in the series. Will there be a change now that you are in charge?'

'No, I'm pretty sure they'll still be critical.' There are a few laughs round the room.

As it has got tighter, the series has become increasingly acrimonious.

'I meant, will there be a change of tactics?'

'Certainly not at the request of the opposition.'

'Do you think the fact that you were the only real option as replacement captain saved you from being dropped?'

Ouch! 'Michael, I don't know what would or wouldn't have been in the selectors' minds if Rob wasn't in hospital. I've been picked to play, so I'll do everything I can as captain and player to make sure we win the Ashes.'

'You've brought Casey Thomas into the squad. Will he be a like-for-like replacement for Rob?'

'Look, we're not ready to tell you the final eleven yet. We are still considering the option of playing an extra bowler. But, clearly, if we don't, then Casey will play. He's a very exciting [*reckless*], young [*immature*] player [*ego*], and if he does play I'm sure he will do a great job for us.' *I'm absolutely not sure of anything of the sort.*

'Thomas is a very stylish batsman. Does his selection represent a desire for the team to play a more attractive "brand" of cricket?'

It's not fucking dressage.

'No, Casey's been picked to score runs.'

A volley of microphones are ranged on me, waiting for

any slip, any unguarded comment. You don't even have to say anything controversial to get into trouble. I was once too vague answering a banal question about contract negotiations, and this was splashed across the back pages the following day as, 'McCall refuses to rule out player strike over pay!'

I don't like these public occasions. I feel a sort of vertigo, as if I'm standing next to a cliff edge. Ever since I was a kid in school chapel services, I've been scared of suddenly doing the worst thing I can imagine. Of shouting out an obscenity during prayers, or laughing loudly during a funeral. My mind plucks at it, can't resist imagining what would happen in toe-curling detail. It's not that I feel in genuine danger of carrying through on it. It's not tempting; just the opposite. It's the sheer proximity of the cliff edge, of being a second's whim away from disaster, which tugs and appals the imagination.

Under the table my knuckles whiten.

'You haven't scored a hundred in nearly eighteen months now. Do you think that puts you under pressure for your place in the side?'

What do you think?

'Like I say, I'm a batsman. My job is to score runs. I haven't been doing that and I need to start soon. Not to keep my place in the side, but to help win games of cricket for England.'

I glance over at the corner of the room to the large, lugubrious form of our team media manager. Jabba takes the hint and lumbers forward. 'OK, gentlemen, I think we'll leave it there.' Additional questions keep coming from the packed room, but with his battered briefcase and even more battered face, he gestures me towards the door and, eyes down, I head through it, as quickly as I can without looking as if I'm fleeing.

'Why do you let all those balls go past, Daddy?'

'What do you mean, Sam?'

'Why do you let all those balls go past without hitting them?' His earnest little voice winds out of the telephone. The line makes him sound even smaller than he is. 'Mummy says it's because you're waiting for the ball to go soft, but I think you should hit them for four instead, that would make it go soft quicker, wouldn't it?'

'That's not a bad idea. Maybe I'll try that. How are you doing Sam? How was school today?'

I know what the answer's going to be before I ask the question. All I can ever get out of him.

'Good.'

My eyes are screwed shut to catch every sound, the phone jammed hard against my ear, as if I can burrow down the wire to get closer to him. 'How was the party on Saturday?'

'Good.'

'Did you have fun?'

'Yes.'

'Good. I'm glad. Can you put your mum on, Sam?'

'OK.'

I hear him calling 'Mummy! Mummy!' in the background, then it goes quiet for a few seconds. He comes back panting. 'She doesn't want to talk to you . . . Gotta go, Daddy.'

'Bye, Sam . . .' But the line is already dead. '. . . love you.'

Love you, Sam.

Jabba and I wander back across the outfield from the press conference.

The ground is having one of its mythically perfect moments.

The clear, untroubled light picks out the leaves on the trees behind the Nursery End.

Lord's is beautiful in the sunshine.

Great white sails on a lush, unblemished sea.

Ahead of us, though, a familiar figure stands like a storm cloud in the middle of the square, glowering down at the pitch.

'Hail to the chief!' The sight of his natural foe causes Jabba to chunter belligerently as he shambles forward.

'I'm sure there are people who like Yorkshiremen,' he mutters irascibly. 'I'm sure there are people who enjoy their company . . . people who don't find them a race of smug, joyless vulgarians—'

'Jabba!' I warn gently.

'I'm sure these people exist and that there are plenty of them.' He pauses, stopping to readjust his bulk. 'I'm just not sure there are that many of them outside Yorkshire,' he concludes acidly.

'You're even more misanthropic than usual this morning, Jabba. Now look out, he's coming over.'

The chief exec marches up to us. 'Morning, Mac,' he says curtly, shaking my hand. He nods coldly at Jabba, no hand offered. Jabba, barely acknowledging the nod, turns away to study the Lord's skyline. The pair's mutual animosity is no secret.

'Big day on Thursday . . . hope you're up to it?'

'We'll do our best.'

'Not good, losing Rob like that. Massive blow for us.'

You don't need to tell me. Rob has been an immense presence all series, a sporting icon at the height of his powers.

'Can't tell you how important this is for all of us . . .' he continues.

'Well . . .'

'. . . for the game, for the country even.'

'Like I say we'll—'

'What's the side going to be? You decided yet?'

'We're probably leaning towards Thomas. He's—'

'Really! Didn't expect that.' He stares at me dubiously. 'You sure? Big match to throw him into . . .'

Jesus, at some point I'm going to get to finish a sentence.

'We think—'

'Other options, you know? More experience.'

'Like I say, we think—'

'Sure you know best. Have you checked that with Rob, though?'

'Yes, he's on board with it.'

'Well . . . OK . . . I see.' He still looks dubious. He opens his mouth to say something, but I've already grabbed the opportunity offered by his momentary hiatus to nod, break away, and head off in the direction of the pavilion. Jabba drops into stride alongside me in silence. I feel like a tugboat escorting a battered old warship.

'You can always tell a Yorkshireman . . .' he says. 'You just can't tell him much.'

I drop into my best Barnsley accent. 'They say what they like, and they like what they bloody well say!' I turn to look at our media manager. 'He really doesn't like *you*, though, does he?'

'*Odi et amo.*'

'No . . . I reckon just hate.'

'Well, you can judge a man by his enemies. So that's a tick in that box for me.'

We start to climb the steps to the pavilion.

'You know one thing I've noticed, Mac,' he rumbles. 'The easiest way to determine your standing in someone's eyes is to observe to what degree they accurately attribute *your* ideas to *you*.

'There's a sliding scale that runs all the way from them giving your ideas to someone else, through appropriating your ideas for themselves, right up to falsely attributing other people's ideas to you. If they hold you in high enough regard, they will tag your name to a thought they want to promote, in the belief that your halo can add a sheen of quality.'

'So where do you fall on our friend's scale, do you think?'

'Ha! I reckon he'd rather credit a fortune cookie than me.' He shrugs. 'Like they say, you can achieve anything if you don't care who gets the credit.'

Tuesday evening

Four of us sit in the bar. Head coach, chief selector, me, Grub. I've asked Grub along so I can't be outvoted. Three beers and a water sit in front of us. I don't waver often these days, but at the moment I would dearly love to swap my water for something stronger.

'So, just to be clear. How *are* the two of you? Is that issue settled?'

I shrug. I played in a match for Middlesex up at Old Trafford last year. Casey and I had a bit of a run-in.

'I can't speak for him. There's no issue at my end.'

'What happened exactly?'

'I was batting with Clarkey. He and Thomas got into it over a bat-pad appeal. Things started to get out of hand; they were nose to nose and screaming at each other in the middle of the pitch. I went over to try and calm things down and Thomas threw a punch at me.' I shrug again.

'I still had my lid on. I think he did himself more damage than me. His own captain sent him off the field and we didn't see him again. He got a six-week ban in the end. As far as I'm concerned, that's all done and forgotten.'

'So you're happy to have him in the team?'

'Yep.'

If Rob were here, we wouldn't even be having this conversation, would we?

'And you're happy that you two aren't going to cause any issues. It's a big match.'

'Look. I can handle Thomas. If it's the right team, it's the right team. Let's put our strongest eleven on the pitch.'

'An' it's not like he's got a history of hittin' 'is own team,' Grub interjects with mock sincerity, 'so you should be fine.'

Tuesday night

I am in bed, reading. Trying to calm my mind. Trying to let the tension slide out of me enough to go to sleep. The pill from the doc sits on the bedside table next to me. I'll use it if I have to, but as a last resort.

My mind is whirling, jumping from one unfinished thought to another.

I watched him signing autographs today. Strutting around in his new England kit. Tall and athletic, with boy-band looks and immaculately fashionable hair. He walked past a group of teenage girls and their eyes followed him, entranced. After he'd gone they turned and mouthed '*Oh my God!*' to each other.

I can't shake the feeling that he is the wrong call. But nor can I tell whether my distrust of him is a result of our history. Casey Thomas would never have been my choice. But others have made the decision. I am just going to have to trust them.

I check the time on my phone, and feel the usual impulse to call Beth. I want to hear her voice, want to tell her, *It will be OK, it won't always be like this.* But it never works out;

I can never find the words. We can talk about the kids now, but little else.

I force myself to focus on the book in my hands, flick through the pages, looking for the one I want. It's a collection I know well. I find the right one, read it from the page, even though I know it by heart.

> *Bright clasp of her whole hand around my finger,*
> *My daughter, as we walk together now.*
> *All my life I'll feel a ring invisibly*
> *Circle this bone with shining: when she is grown*
> *Far from today as her eyes are far already.*

Ten minutes later, my eyelids droop, the book slides from my hand. I flick off the light and turn over. Darkness swallows the room.

And there they are.

I often find them here. Just as I start to let go. As my mind makes that first sideways slide out of full consciousness.

They wait for me in the shadowlands, on the borders of sleep. Not as they are now, but as I remember them best, two years younger. Faces, smiling one moment, then impossibly earnest.

As from the start, their smallest movements open my chest to the elements, my flawed heart bruised by each glance and gesture.

'Come, Daddy. Come,' arms outstretched. I reach for them. Hands, tinier than rain on my skin, pluck at my fingers. Then, turning, they lead me, baby-stepped, down into the dark.

Friday 2.23 p.m.

Australia	348 all out (119 overs)
England	24 for 2 (7.5 overs)

The rest of them are chuckling, looking past me to the silent TV screen in the corner of the room. I follow their eyes and groan.

A couple of years ago I was out of shape, and considerably heavier than I am now. On the screen is some old footage of me scoring runs. It is from my 'fat phase'. I'm playing well – I remember the innings, I get a hundred – but I look decidedly chunky and, as I take my helmet off and lift my arms aloft, the difference between my face and the younger, chubbier one on the screen is comical.

'Wow,' Grub drawls in his thick Geordie, 'lookin' a tad low in the water there, mate.'

'Sell that diet, Mac,' comes a voice from the back of the room. 'You'll make millions!'

'The camera adds ten pounds, remember,' I say smiling.

'That right, is it?' Grub asks ingenuously. 'So, just how many cameras are on you there, Mac?'

We are still laughing when it happens – the bowler runs in and bowls; the batsman plays what looks like a firm push back down the pitch, but behind him the wicket explodes.

17

The fielders erupt, instantly followed by every Aussie in the ground.

I flick to the replay on the screen. Good ball. Nice length, and it's just nipped back up the slope into the top of middle-and-off.

Right then, Mac.

I slip on helmet and gloves, hop out of the chair, and spend a few seconds trying to get my feet moving.

'Go well, Mac.'

'Dig in, mate.'

'Good luck, Jimbo.'

I am out of the dressing-room door and down the stairs. Paintings of the game's Greats stare down at me; my spikes clash on the hard stairs; down into the Long Room, lines of faces turning to look. Voices bounce around me, wishing me well, urging me on.

As usual, on the way to the crease my heart is properly ticking. It never goes away this; never gets much less than it was the first time. Pulse racing, blood pounding.

My mind gets quieter. From the moment the helmet goes on, it switches to the job at hand, becomes stiller. Released from the torture of waiting, it gets calmer.

But my body doesn't. It gears up for the first ball like it's a fight to the death, gives it the kitchen sink during the walk to the middle. Adrenaline, testosterone – you name it, it's flowing. I'm shivering slightly from the force of it as I take guard. My hands trembling a little as I settle the bat into my grip. *Not nerves, excitement*, I tell myself.

I take a deep breath . . . long and slow . . . and then I look round. And, just for a moment, I can pause to take in where I am.

The Test

God, I love this!

The full crowd is buzzing. The ground hums like a living thing. Every pair of eyes is on the middle. Thirty thousand people. And for each and every person there, a hundred more are at home glued to the screen. And for every viewer in England, there's another one sitting in the dark of an Australian night, not to mention the millions of neutrals in dozens of other countries. At this moment, I feel like I'm standing at the centre of the world.

We are in a real hole. We are scrapping to survive in the game and the series. We are in danger of surrendering the Ashes here and now.

But this is who I am, and this is what I do. *Time to go to work.*

Now the routine kicks in. I get my feet moving, bend, flex, check the fielders' positions, my movements crisp, business-like.

I recheck my guard with the umpire, prod a few marks on the wicket, walk away a few steps, then return to the crease.

I take one last look round at the fielders and drop into my stance. Fifty yards away, the bowler settles the ball in his hand, starts walking, then running, accelerates towards me. The hum of the crowd turns into a mounting roar as the Aussies in the stands cheer him into the wicket.

Right, come on Mac. Let's do this. Come on . . . See ball, hit ball.

The noise crescendoes as the bowler reaches the crease, and then explodes upwards as the fielders appeal. The ball has pitched just outside off-stump, jagged back up the hill and hit me on the knee-roll. The fielders are howling as one man at the umpire, their arms outstretched, eyes bulging, and their roar is echoed by their supporters in the stands. For a second, I think I'm safe. Then the umpire nods fractionally, and his arm slowly swings forward and upwards.

Out, LBW, first ball.

The Australians charge inwards, feral in their joy, leaping all over each other. Their sections of the stands are going crazy. My stomach has fallen away, dropped through the pitch and kept going.

For a batsman, getting out is a sudden and violent thing. Unlike most losses in sport, which are more gradual, it happens in an instant. You are in, and then, the next moment, you are out. Evicted from the scene, your meaningful role in the match is over.

It could be your first ball or your four-hundredth. Few sporting failures come so fast, and with no advance warning. Breaking down in a grand prix, a runner pulling a hamstring, conceding a last-gasp winning try in a rugby match – these are parallels, but they are rare and extreme occurrences rather than typical.

I play one part. I am a batsman.

I have one real job, one role to perform of any substance.

Yet, it is perfectly possible that in a Test match that lasts five days, my opportunities to perform that job could be limited to one ball. Confined to the four-tenths of a second it takes for a delivery to travel from hand to stumps.

Or, I could be on the pitch for almost the whole five days, in an exhausting, mind-sapping trial of stamina, concentration and skill.

Or more likely, more often, somewhere in between.

Wednesday afternoon

'Hi Jabba.'

'Mac.' I stop. There's an off-note there. The pause slightly too long, the reply overly casual. I retrace my steps to his open door. He clicks his mouse hurriedly, clearing his screen, and looks up.

Hmmm. 'What are you writing there, Jabba?'

He tries to look insouciant. It's not an expression his walrus face is particularly good at.

'Oh, you know ... words,' he says.

I wait, letting the pause lengthen into a silence.

He adjusts his twenty-stone bulk. The chair creaks underneath him. 'Moving them around, putting them in order.'

I wait.

'Then rearranging them.'

I stare at him. *I'm not going anywhere, Jabba.*

'Then going back to the first arrangement,' he drawls, 'because although it's far from perfect, it's a damn sight better than the shitty second version,' he chuckles.

I've never seen him look uncomfortable before, ever. The reason can't be good news.

'What sort of words?'

'Nouns, verbs . . . mostly. The odd unnecessary adjective.'

'What is it, Jabba?'

'Nothing you need to worry about, Mac.'

'Jabba!'

He sighs heavily, 'Sorry, Mac. The MD wants a media plan in place in case we lose. I was just scribbling some notes.'

'Jesus! We haven't bowled a ball yet.'

'I know, I know. Well, you know what they're like, professional arse-coverers. They didn't get where they are today by not diving for cover at the first sign of trouble.'

'Be nice if they showed a little faith.'

'Not sure they know the meaning of the word.'

'Well then, put it in there.' I turn to leave. '*The substance of things hoped for, the evidence of things not seen.*'

Friday 2.31 p.m.

It felt like it might have done too much. I'd got a decent stride in. The ball still had a fair distance to travel to get to the stumps. I walk down the pitch to the tall figure of Casey Thomas at the other end.

'Was that sliding down, do you think?'

He shrugs. 'Dunno.'

'Worth a review?'

He shrugs again, says nothing.

Thanks Casey, big help.

The seconds are ticking by.

It didn't feel out, but it's hard to overturn decisions once they're given. Reviews are precious, don't want to waste one.

Gotta decide, gotta decide.

The umpire is looking at me, wanting a decision.

Time's up, now or never.

I bring my arms up into the T-shape for a referral; the umpire presses his earpiece and starts talking to the third umpire upstairs. The twelfth men arrive with drinks. I take a sip, out of reflex rather than thirst – I've only been out here for a single ball, after all. On the big screen the Hawk-Eye replay is unfolding: RED, pitched outside off, RED, hitting in line, GREEN, sliding down and missing the leg stump by the tiniest of margins.

I breathe again. Put my lid on and go back to the crease.

'Lucky bastard,' MacKenzie mutters at me from short leg.

I shrug back at him and grin.

DAY TWO

Like a tremor in an earthquake region, a wicket runs as a shiver through a batting team's dressing room. There can't be *no* reaction; someone has to pick up their helmet, be wished well, and walk out into the sunshine. But nor do you want *too much* response. Gasps and swearing help no one, and unsettle the already nervous. In general, conversations pause, observe a moment's silence, then continue, a little subdued.

Any wicket carries the threat of more. You're at your most vulnerable at the start of an innings, as your reflexes adjust to the conditions. So wickets have a natural tendency to fall in clumps. And once they start to fall, there is never a guarantee that they'll stop. If three or more go quickly, suddenly you can find yourself in the middle of a genuine collapse.

When you are batting, you win the game slowly, by inches. It takes hours of diligence and skill to wrest supremacy from the opposition. But you can lose it fast. A strong position, battled for and built over two or three days, can be swept away in forty minutes of mayhem.

Collapses have their own momentum. And it feels unstoppable to a team in its grip. The room becomes hushed. The atmosphere moves from relaxed and convivial,

29

the knockabout fun of a happy dressing room, through stages of nervous hope, then edgy chatter, to quiet desperation. The seven stages of the grieving process played out in miniature as a side collapses. It gets quieter and quieter, as the room slowly fills up with guys who've just failed in front of millions, and those who are facing the imminent prospect of doing so.

Walking to the middle as the wickets are clattering, and the crowd is buzzing, is one of the great tests the game has to offer. Mental resilience, sound technique, the ability to trust yourself, your skills, your instincts: these are your only protection, your walls against the raging tide that would swamp you.

If in doubt, simplify. Peel it all back . . .

See ball, hit ball, switch off.

See ball, hit ball, switch off.

One ball at a time.

Just get to the end of the over.

It will get easier.

This too shall pass.

And then . . . slowly at first . . . the pressure eases a fraction. The two batsmen in the middle have managed to staunch the bleeding.

The panic ebbs, the conversations start up again. The bowlers who were doing the damage have tired and had to be changed and, as they settle, the batters are able to counterattack.

The ball starts to hit the middle of the bat, and slowly the pressure is tilted back on to the fielding side.

Friday 2.51 p.m.

Australia	348 all out (119 overs)
England	38 for 4 (12 overs)

There is silence when I walk back in through the dressing-room door.

I lasted another ten balls, and then nicked one to the keeper. There wasn't much I could do. Just one of those balls you need to be lucky enough to miss. I wasn't.

I take off my pads, grab a bottle of water from the fridge, and head out on to the balcony to see if the next pair can stop the rot. Casey has barely managed to put bat on ball, and is looking completely out of his depth.

I overhear two of the bowlers whispering behind me.

'Fuck's sake.'

'I know.'

'We could be bowling again *tonight*, here.'

As I sit down, the tall Lancastrian drives at a wide one. The ball flashes away at head height through the vacant cover region, two bounces and it thuds into the boundary boards. The crowd roars, pleased to have something to cheer about, but it's a poor shot in the circumstances. He's flayed at it on the up, with no control over the stroke. He could easily have nicked it to the waiting slips, or found a fielder in the ring.

31

'Easy, Casey lad,' Grub mutters to himself next to me.

The next ball is similar, and Casey flails at this one as well, missing entirely. The slips leap in anticipation of an edge, and then drop their hands to their heads as a man. The fielders in the ring have crowded in to within a few yards of the figure at the crease. You can't hear them from here, but it's clear they are chattering away. Making sure Casey knows all about the play and miss.

There are hard times to bat, and easy times. Conditions fluctuate during a Test. At the moment, the ball is still fairly new, and swinging around under heavy clouds. Their best bowlers are bowling, and have their tails up because of the wickets we've lost. But they can't bowl for ever: eventually they'll have to be replaced; the ball will get older and easier to play. Conditions will swing in favour of the batsmen. But only if we can weather this storm. We desperately need the pair at the crease to rein themselves in and see off the opening bowlers. Tighten their defence, only play when they have to; protect their wickets and the batsmen still left in the pavilion at all costs. The whole match may hinge on it.

If the forecast is right, tomorrow will be sunny. If we can get to the close of play with wickets in hand then we'll be able to make the most of what are likely to be perfect batting conditions on Saturday. Get ourselves back level in the match, or close to it.

Grub curses under his breath as Casey pushes hard at another wide one. The ball slides off the face of his bat and looks as if it's going to be caught by the fielder at point, but it just dips a little at the last moment and bounces in front of him, safe by a matter of inches.

The Test

The fielders are almost beside themselves with excitement and frustration. They know the match, and the Ashes, are here for the taking: a couple more wickets exposes our tail.

There's one ball to go in the over.

Grub looks up at the screen. Casey's various false shots are being shown one after the other. The replays, in excruciating slow motion, make his batting look pretty ugly. Grub shakes his head.

'Poor lad. Slow motion doesn't half make you look like a wanker.'

It does if you go in and swing like a rusty gate.

'Come on, lad. Just get out of the over,' Grub mutters imploringly. 'Couple more overs and these two'll be off.'

The ball is dug in short. *Leave it, Case.* But he hooks at it, tries to smash it away square of the wicket. The ball flies off the top edge of his bat and sails upwards towards fine leg. *Down ball! Down!* I'm desperately urging the red leather in my head, but fine leg is racing in and covers the ground easily to pouch the catch. The Aussies race across the outfield to him, engulfing him in hugs and high-fives.

I'm holding my face expressionless; the cameras are on me waiting for a reaction, my face huge on the big screen. It looks calm, shows nothing. But my heart has dropped away into an abyss. If I'm honest, I don't really see a way out of this for us now.

But the umpires are holding Casey in the middle. They want to check the bowler's front foot for a no-ball. They talk into their radios. Up on the screen, we see the magnified shot of the popping crease and the bowler's foot inching down towards it, agonisingly slowly. *Jesus, this is going to be tight, you know.* The foot lands and it's right on the line; you can't see anything behind. And since the line belongs to the umpire . . .

'No-ball,' says someone behind me. 'Definitely no-ball!'

The giant foot toggles backwards and forwards, lifting off and on, off and on. The crowd are making their feelings clear. They are cheering like it's a foregone conclusion. 'No-ball!' voices are shouting from the stands. Casey has made his mind up as well. He's put his helmet back on and walked back to re-mark his guard.

'Definitely a no-ball,' someone says again behind me.

I don't know. It couldn't be tighter; there *could* be the tiniest fraction of his boot just touching down behind the line, but then in the next frame there isn't and it's a clear no-ball. You can see these either way.

You pays your money and you takes your choice. It all depends on how the third umpire sees it.

The umpires in the middle have their hands to their ear-pieces. The crowd are getting restless. The giant boot moves up and down. The ground holds its breath.

Then the umpire lifts his finger. OUT. The stands groan in dismay. Grub picks up his bat and gloves and heads out of the room.

A minute later Casey explodes through the door of the dressing room, red-faced and incandescent with fury.

'Bullshit! Bullshit!' He hurls his bat into the corner. It crashes against the panelling. 'Fuckin' bullshit!' Helmet and gloves follow the bat. He is yelling at the top of his voice. The MCC members below us are turning their heads to stare up at the balcony.

I push the balcony doors closed to keep the sounds of his tantrum inside, but can still hear his full-voiced rant against the umpires, their parentage and the Australian nation in general. Hopefully his accent and the closed doors are gar-bling the worst of his language. The last thing he needs is to be answering media questions about his behaviour halfway through his debut. And the last thing we need is any more bad press; we're going to cop it tonight as it is.

Friday 3.40 p.m.

Australia	348 all out (119 overs)
England	110 for 6 (25 overs)

We are through the recognised batsmen now. But this brings our off-spinner to the crease. He is a handy player who bats pretty well, with a few first-class hundreds to his name. He and Grub manage to make it through to tea without further loss, and even start to counterattack as the sun pokes through the clouds.

There is a flurry of boundaries as the ball flies through and over the attacking fields still deployed by the Australians, and the mood in the dressing room has buoyed a little as we go into tea at 110 for 6.

During the interval there is a display of junior cricket and the outfield swarms with young kids in brightly coloured outfits. Those in the crowd who have stayed in the stands are cheering them on. I am sitting with Jabba on the balcony watching. Our resident cynic looks moodier than ever in his crumpled brown suit.

Behind me, Grub is muling Tayls. 'Did you know that the brighter you are, the faster you can rearrange letters in your head?'

'What do you mean?'

The Test

'Well, it's a classic intelligence test. I'll give you a letter and you have to give me the previous one in the alphabet. The faster you can do it, the smarter you are.'

'Go on then.'

'Are you ready . . . ? G.'

'. . . F.'

'Not bad . . . W.'

'Err . . . X, no V.'

'One more . . . U.'

'T,' he says, and for a fraction of a second is pleased with himself until the orders come flying in:

'Yes please, milk one sugar.'

'Coffee, please.'

'Very kind of you, Tayls.'

'Yes, I'll have one.'

He drops his head in resignation and walks towards the kettle.

From our bench, Jabba stares mournfully down at the proceedings below.

'When I was younger, I thought I hated children,' he eventually drawls. 'Then I got older – ' he shifts in his seat – 'and I realised I hated everybody.'

Grub and I laugh.

'As Larkin nearly said,' the big man concedes. 'I'm not joking you know. Well, OK . . .' he adds lugubriously '. . . not *absolutely* everyone.

'But children appal me,' he carries on grumpily. 'Their perfection appals me. Not that they aren't sweet enough. They are. But they are so immaculate, so perfectly formed. The thought that we all started like that, and descend . . . to this.' He waves a hand in the general direction of his fleshy folds. And indeed, looking at him now, the morbidly overweight veteran of a dozen foreign wars, and a thousand legendary lunches, it is hard to believe he was once like the kids in the colourful T-shirts below.

I know better, though.

'Grub, have you ever seen Jabba in his heyday?' I ask. When he shakes his head, I pop inside, borrow an iPad from the team analyst and quickly manage to pull up a photo I found on the internet a few months ago. In the background are military vehicles, rice paddies and a jungle somewhere in South-East Asia. In the foreground is a young war correspondent. I pass it across.

Grub's jaw literally drops. He looks up at Jabba speechlessly, then back down at the photo. Jabba groans.

'OK, Mac. No need to remind me. These days I look like I'm robbing a bank in a rubber mask of my own face.'

Greg, our Strength and Conditioning coach, sticks his head out of the door at that moment. 'Mac, I'm just heading over to the Nursery ground to do a power session,' he says. Then he grins: 'You can come too, if you like, Jabba.'

The old soak snorts in amusement.

'I know. You've told me. Twenty minutes of exercise a day and I could add years of discomfort to my life. Thanks,' he drawls, 'but I'll pass.'

Grub is still looking at the photo. He hands it up to the S&C. 'Who's this?' Greg asks. I point at Jabba, and the reaction from our fitness coach is, if anything, even more extreme than Grub's.

The grinning young journalist in the photo is about the most handsome man I've ever seen. It's not a lucky photo, either; I've asked people who knew him, and they confirmed it. Jabba used to be absolutely stunning. Women would walk into traffic when he went past.

Finally regaining the power of speech, Grub asks what, to his mind, is the obvious next thought, 'Howay man! Just how many women did you sleep with?'

'None who wouldn't deny it now,' Jabba says briskly. The bell sounds below as he says it. 'Anyway, the umpires have gone; back to work, Grub.'

Grub heads inside to grab his gear. Greg bends down and picks up his kit bag. 'Well, I'll be over on the Nursery ground with all my – ' he holds up the bag – 'apparati,' he says, looking pleased with himself, 'so if you change your mind, Jabba . . .'

'The plural of apparatus is apparatus, in English *and* Latin,' Jabba replies without missing a beat. 'Don't try to be clever, Greg, doesn't suit you.'

The balcony empties, leaving me alone with Jabba. He is trying to twist his features into something approaching sympathy.

'You might get a chance to use that media plan after all,' I say grimly.

He snorts and mutters an obscenity.

'I had a shit in head office the other day,' he drawls, 'and on the back of the cubicle door someone had written: *500 people work for the ECB. At this exact moment in time, you are the only one of them who knows exactly what he is doing.*'

'Is there any chance that you wrote that, Jabba?'

His vast face aims at an expression of wounded innocence. 'Now do you think I would do a thing like that?'

The Australians are making their way back on to the field. Around us Lord's hums gently, like a vast hive.

'Jabba?' I ask. He lifts his eyebrows at me. 'Do you ever think maybe it's not the chief exec?' He scowls. 'And that maybe it's not the *bastard hacks*?'

'Maybe it's just . . . you know – ' he's looking confused – 'too much booze . . . too much rich food . . . not enough regular exercise?'

Now he is glaring at me.

He levers himself off the bench and looms over me. 'James McCall, if you can suggest a better way for me to drink myself into an early grave, then I'd be happy to hear it,' he growls down at me, before breaking into a grin. 'Besides, that sounds suspiciously like common sense and perspective. And you know my feelings about that sort of thinking.'

After tea, the wickets fall steadily again.

Grub is being his usual irritating self to the opposition. Busy between the wickets, he steals singles where there aren't any, puts pressure on the fielders and turns ones into twos. He is also taking the bowlers on, knocking them off their lengths and riding his luck, with a mixture of lusty blows and miscues that hurry our total along at a brisk clip.

But he is getting little or no help from the other end. None of our bowlers can get much of a toehold when they get out to the middle. It is not easy batting at the moment, and each of them has looked at sea while out there and has departed soon after.

Our senior fast bowler is lying propped half upright in the centre of the dressing room. His massive frame dwarfs that of everyone else in the room. We have played nearly fifty Tests together, and that's about the same number of things I've heard him say in that time.

He and Rob are the main reasons we are still in this series. He has been immense throughout the summer, and was again in the first innings here, taking six wickets and keeping the touring side's batsmen in check almost single-handedly.

41

His knee is buggered, has been for weeks, but he has insisted on playing on regardless.

Since his heroics this morning he has been on the physio bed, leg encased in ice, watching the TV screen impassively as the wickets tumble. He shows very little, and says even less. When the eighth wicket falls, he prises himself upright, rips the ice from his leg and limps heavily over to his kit bag in the corner. I don't know what to say.

God, he deserved better from the rest of us.

I walk across to where he is strapping his pads on. His huge limbs make the furniture look child-sized.

'Go well, Oak. Hang in there, bat for Grub.' I pat him on the back.

He grunts in reply. And then as I walk away he mutters something under his breath. It sounds like 'fuckin' shithouse'. I think it's aimed at the world in general, rather than me. I hope so, anyway.

'Bowling pills please, doc,' he says quietly, hand out-stretched. He takes his usual handful of anti-inflammatories and painkillers, swallows them without water, then sits back and waits for the next wicket to fall.

If it wasn't for Grub, this would be a full-scale rout, and as it is we are all out for 179 when he top-edges an attempted pull shot and is caught for 78.

I tap him on the back as he sits down next to me and starts taking his pads off, 'Batted, mate!'

He nods in acknowledgement.

'Thanks,' but he looks sombre. 'We been gut-shot here?'

It's crossed my mind, but I'm not ready to say it out loud.

'Maybe not. Not if we can get into them tonight. And

there's weather around days four and five. We're not dead yet.'

But we are on the critical list.

Grub strips off his shirt and slumps back against the wall behind us. I smile, because it is extraordinary. 'That's not one you're putting on your CV is it, Greg?' I say to our S&C, nodding at Grub. Despite being a full-time sportsman, and not living all that badly, Grub has managed to retain a physique that seems to have been fashioned from cold mashed potato.

'Ah know,' Grub says, looking down at his pasty torso. 'I've the body of a forty-five-year-old Glaswegian drunk.'

'I love you, Grub, but to be honest, if I found you in a trawler net, I'd throw you back in.' I laugh. 'I reckon you may well represent the Everest of strength and conditioning training.'

'Nah, give me six months: I'll have him on the cover of *Men's Fitness*,' Greg says confidently.

'Really? What, as the *Before* photo?'

High, high in the Chinese hills, there was once a monastery where a distinguished Taoist guru lived with his disciples.

In the evenings the monks would gather in the Great Hall to listen to their leader's teachings and to meditate. But there was a stray cat that had adopted the monastery, and each evening it would follow the monks into the hall. It would mewl, scratch, and generally be annoying throughout their silent meditation.

It did this every night until the great teacher became so irritated by it that he told his followers to put a collar on the cat and tether it on the far side of the monastery each evening.

This worked well and, for a while, teacher, cat and monks all went through their nightly routine.

One day, the learned teacher died. But the monks continued to tie up the cat each evening.

More years passed.

And eventually the cat died.

So the monks went down to the nearest village, found a replacement cat, and tied it up each evening instead.

Two centuries later, religious scholars write learned essays on the importance of tying up a cat prior to evening meditation.

This is how much of cricket works.

Test matches suck you in.

Unlike most sports matches, they live alongside you for a while. Like a book you are reading, you can put them down, go about your day, then pick them up again. They have their own narrative arc, independent of your life, but long enough lived so as to weave themselves into a short section of it. Test series even more so. They can accompany a whole summer. They ignore the classical unities, and sprawl their story across a wider canvas.

When I was at school, the best of all possible days was the Thursday at the start of a Test during the holidays. I would roll out of bed, especially early at 10.30 or so, and have my breakfast ready in front of me for the first ball of the day's play.

What bliss, what unfettered joy to have no other calls on my time, and five days lying in front of the TV stretching ahead of me. If I missed a single ball of a Test summer, it was a disappointment.

I don't imagine it's the same now. There is always something on – and countless channels of 24-hour sport if you have SKY.

★

We had started the series well two months ago by winning the first Test in Cardiff.

Then the second Test was a washout.

We dominated the third Test and were heading for an Ashes-securing win, when we suddenly collapsed on the last day. We eventually clung on for a draw, the last pair surviving for three overs to see us safe. But that seemed to be the turning point for the series.

At Headingley, in the fourth Test, we were blown away. We lost by a huge margin and, even worse, lost our captain and leading run-scorer to a burst appendix halfway through the match.

Lord's would normally be the second Test of a major series, but the usual dates for this match clashed with a global economic summit in London. The resulting security concerns forced the ECB to schedule it as the final Test of the series.

So we've arrived here 1-1 for the final instalment. We hold the Ashes, therefore a draw will be good enough for us to retain the urn. If the Aussies win, they'll head home with it.

Lord's, the Home of Cricket and my home ground, is a fittingly iconic venue for the finale of a series that has captured the public imagination, both in England and around the world.

They've played this game here for over two hundred years. Stumps were first pitched here the year before Waterloo. It is hard to see now what it must have looked like all that time ago. It was seventy years later when the first Test match was played here. There are paintings of it on the wall, but it is unrecognisable. It is impossible to superimpose them over the modern stands and corporate boxes. Only the old pavilion remains largely the same.

Two hundred years of civilisation have softened and smoothed sport and ground alike. The wild turf has been tamed, meticulously metric'd and millimetred. This strip of grass, tended for decade after decade, has been rolled, watered, cut, fertilised, repaired, and rolled some more; decade after decade after century. Acres of grass are now immaculate to the last blade, like some vast baize tabletop.

At the same time, the rough, disreputable sport has also been tamed, civilised and dragged into the nation's heartland. Cricket started, like horse racing and prizefighting, as an excuse for gambling. And, like the other two, hasn't moved that far since, although it hides the fact slightly better. But for a while it came to represent more: to be not only typically English, but also England's quintessence, its very soul.

How is it that this game, its roots sunk so far into England's deep, fertile soil, became global?

How did it make the transition to the bone-hard earth of the Australian outback, to the rich, crumbling clay of the subcontinent, to the African high veldt and the beaches of the Caribbean?

How did it become richer, finer, and more beloved in the translation? Because, for every idea of cricket that England sent out, its Commonwealth sent back tenfold.

And though the bacon-and-egg ties sat here in their hubris, and thought themselves Lords of *their* game, the truth was that its spirit had already flown, away on the trade winds, to sunnier and more vibrant lands.

Now we are become a land poor in our own currency, keepers of relics for those who have *real* power in the game.

and though
We are not now that strength which in old days
Moved earth and heaven, that which we are, we are;

This Lord's.

This England.

This game.

Its roots sunk so deep, so entwined with our ideas of ourselves.

And now the old ground sits here, heavy under a brooding sky. The chill in the air is matched by the sombre mood of the crowd. There is a foretaste of autumn about the late-summer nip: dampness, decay, and endings.

I look down at the pitch, wondering what it has in store for us.

Is there another sport that has a living, changing thing at its heart?

While cricket is a contest between two teams of eleven players, there is always a third force out there on the field of play. Unknown and unpredictable, but with at least an equal hand in the way the match unfolds.

Even the best groundsman cannot, hand-on-heart, tell you how a pitch will play. And only the worst would try to prophesy its progress over five full days.

Whatever it looks like on the first morning, only one thing is certain: it will not stay constant. The grass will continue to grow. The sun will dry it, the rain will moisten it, the players will scar it and mark it. Brushes and rollers, light and heavy, will have their debatable impacts. It will change and evolve. The styles of play it favours will vary.

It is the factor that tips us towards Art and away from Science. The unseen element, which scrambles order, confuses plans, and rolls the dice afresh each and every time we pick a team or set a field.

I see Jabba outside alone on the balcony; he is hunched over with his eyes closed, leaning against the rail and grimacing in obvious pain. I stick my head round the door.

'You OK, Jabba?'

'Yep, fine.' He manages a grin. 'Just practising for when I'm not.'

'Jabba . . .'

'I'm fine. Go on, get on with it.' He nods towards the pitch. 'Go.'

Reluctantly, I leave him. As I pass the doctor in the dressing room I pause. 'Just check on Jabba, will you?' I say to him under my breath.

Friday 5.48 p.m.

| Australia | 348 (119 overs) |
| England | 179 (43 overs) |

When you go out to field in a Test match at Lord's, the members line the stairs, and cram themselves in on either side of you. The winding route down from the first floor, through the Long Room and out on to the field is narrowed almost to the width of a fast bowler's shoulders.

It starts as applause as the captain comes out of the dressing room, hundreds of hands creating a cacophony in the enclosed space that drowns out the clatter of our spikes on the floor. Then, as the team files out of the door and trots down the steps, the blazer-and-tied throng becomes a football terrace, a full-throated roar of exhortation.

Come on, lads!

Go on, England!

Good luck, Mac!

Like fanatics driving the peloton up the mountain.

Feet stamp the floor, hands slap shoulders. The noise swells and swells, and whoever you are, whatever you've done, wherever you've played, the hairs on the back of your neck prick up, goose bumps swarm over you and your heart races.

And then we reach the Long Room and loud becomes deafening. The members who have waited and jostled to get close to the players' route don't waste their moment. Face after face leans into you, exhorting; goading – momentary flashes of individual support in a tidal wave of noise and animation. Through the doors, down the steps, and the team surges out on to the field like a boxer entering the ring. And then there comes the answering roar from the stands, as our white-clad figures run out on to the green turf.

I set the field, throw the ball to Oak, and take my position at first slip next to Grub.

Right then: it's now or never, fellas.

From the first over, it is clear that our bowlers are not ready to hand the Ashes over yet. Tired and sore they may be, but they come racing in and hurl everything they have at the Australian batsmen.

Oak in particular has rolled back the years and is producing a vintage spell. He beats the bat again and again, and pummels the batsmen around the hands and body. He has at least one knee that urgently requires the surgeon's knife, and may force him into retirement at the end of the summer, but nevertheless he is bowling like a force of nature, as well as I've ever seen him bowl.

He walks slowly, limping heavily on the way back to his mark. But if he is in as much agony as our physio reckons, then he doesn't show it each time he wheels round and comes charging in again.

I am in awe of our bowlers. There are days when their sacrifice is akin to self-harm. But still they come. You throw them the ball, and in they run.

The Test

The medics have been patching Oak up all summer. Again and again getting one last match out of him. He was scheduled for surgery after the third Test, if the Ashes were retained. But then we fluffed our lines, and so he had to play in the fourth match, at Headingley. We lost there, and so here he is again, virtually on one leg, not knowing if his career is over, but still running in hard all the same.

He is an awesome sight, terrifying for the batsman. It is like having a house running in to bowl at you. And with a new ball in his hand and the crowd around him, he is every inch the bowler who has taken two hundred Test wickets. Skilful and fast, his height making the ball rear awkwardly off fullish lengths. He hits one of the openers on the back hip; the ball misses the padding and thuds sickeningly into bone. The batsman crumples to the ground under the force of it, but pushes himself straight back up from the turf and limps away towards square leg.

The next ball squeezes straight through his defence and clips the bails. We whoop in celebration and charge in to where Oak is standing in the centre of the pitch, his head thrown back in a cathartic roar of pain and triumph.

When the new batsman arrives, he is immediately hit on the hand, the ball ripping his bottom thumb off the handle. It takes their physio nearly ten minutes to determine that he can carry on. But eventually he does.

Should I add another slip fielder to the cordon?

This is do-or-die stuff for us here; it may be our last chance to force our way back into the match, and to do that we need wickets. On the other hand, we have the batsmen under pressure and the last thing we need is to gift them easy runs and let them get away.

And then, just as my mind is distracted, agonising over possible tactical changes, the edge comes.

I see it late, am slow to move as a result, and the ball flashes quick, low and hard to my left hand. It surprises me, and so, fatally, my first movement is to tighten up, flinch slightly. Just when I need to be loose and relaxed, I tense. The world seems to slow down. I am moving, reaching, straining to get my hand down to it. But even as I'm moving, I know I'm too late, I'm not going to get there. I'm going to miss the chance – maybe our last chance – of getting back into the match.

Then the ball slams into a hand, but it isn't mine. Grub has dived full-length across me and taken a brilliant one-handed catch. He lands in a roll and is back to his feet in one movement, grinning back at me. I could kiss him.

'Sorry, Mac, didn't think it was gonna carry.'

I shake my head as I hug him. 'It was, but I wasn't going to get there.'

The crowd is roaring around us.

We jog up the pitch, exchange high-fives with Oak and the others. Suddenly there is energy in the group, excitement – hope, even.

Could this be the start of something special? Can we turn the tables, get the pressure back on them and keep the wickets falling? Maybe get a target we can chase in the fourth innings?

The Aussies are wobbling here at 5 for 2. They have a horrible forty minutes left to bat now before the close of play. Their dressing room will be distinctly jittery. They are still well ahead in the match, but we've definitely got them on the ropes at the moment. Our opening bowlers are all over their batsmen. If we can just make it tell. Two more wickets now and anything could happen.

The Test

*

There is something special about the way Grub catches a ball.

Our wicketkeeping coach calls it 'the gift'.

Most keepers catch well in training. Their feet move deftly, their balance is good, they watch the ball all the way into their hands. You can fire ball after ball at them in training and it all works. Fluid, confident, consistent.

Grub has the gift that a few have, but most don't. He can do it just the same in the cauldron of a Test match. When he keeps in a match, the stumps and the bat and the other players, and the stands with their 30,000 people, and the TV cameras, are not there.

It's just him, and the ball.

Standing next to him for a whole day's play, you can only marvel at his consistency. Ball after ball, hour after hour, the ball seems to melt into his gloves. Each makes the same sound: solid, comforting, and unchanging.

And the edge, when it comes, never seems to surprise him, or catch him off balance. He is never caught with his feet in clay, having to grab awkwardly or hurriedly. On the contrary, however sharp the chance, he looks as if he was somehow expecting it. Never seems to see it late, always seems to have time.

Just him, and the ball.

That's the gift.

India, twelve years ago

I joined my first Lions tour as a late call-up, and intercepted the rest of the squad in a Jaipur hotel.

After a twenty-hour journey, I arrive an hour or so after the others and drag myself upstairs, exhausted and excited in equal measures.

When I find my way to the right room, the door is already open. I shoulder my way inside, suitcases in hand, and find my new roommate sitting on the edge of the bed in a towel.

'Arlreet, lad,' he says cheerfully, and then in what sounds to me like a string of random noises, 'd'ya knurr howta git tha footy on this?'

His arm is outstretched towards the antique TV screen in the corner, apparently trying to squeeze the remote control to death.

I am looking at the double bed he is sitting on. 'Is there only the one bed?'

'Aye, 'fraid so,' he grins lopsidedly at me. 'Shotgun being the big spoon.'

He laughs at the look on my face.

'Am afraid I do snore a bit.' He points to his nose. 'Broke

ma conk when I was a kid; can't breathe through it properly.'
He goes back to working the TV for a moment before
relenting.

'Nah, I'm just joshing. Don't worry, lad. Ah phoned down
to reception, they said they'd sort it.' For a second I think
he's still talking about his snoring, but then I catch on. His
accent is almost comically thick.

Reading my mind, he adds, 'Though, to be honest, neither
of us could understand a word the other was saying.'

As if on cue, there is a knock behind me and a man
appears in the open doorway carrying an ice bucket on a
tray.

'Hi,' I say.

'Ice, sir?'

'I'm sorry?'

'You order ice?'

I look back over my shoulder at the semi-naked Geordie
crossing the room with a big grin.

He looks at the tray and the ice bucket. 'Well, I wasn't
hopeful, like,' he laughs. 'Don't worry, Mac, the bed's yours,
I don't mind sleeping in the bath.'

Then he holds out his hand. 'Grub, by the way. Nice to
meet you.'

Friday 6.19 p.m.

Australia	348 and 23 for 2 (11 overs)
England	179 all out

'Come on, fellas, here we go! Great work, Oak! Brilliant, mate. Let's get behind him, fellas.'

Grub is next to me, chirping away as usual. He is a ball of energy in the field, constantly bouncing and encouraging; endlessly exhorting the bowlers and fielders to greater levels of focus and commitment.

He is working twice as hard in this match, because he is missing the other half of his double-act. Rob would normally be here too, an explosion of athleticism and commitment, leading by example, lodestone to our lesser mettle. He and Grub are the heartbeat of our fielding.

'Ooh! Outstanding that from you, Ben! Love that, mate!' Grub cheers as the ball beats the bat again. He flicks the ball sideways to Tayls at second slip, and turns to him. 'Come on then, what 'ave you got for us, Tayls lad?'

Tayls ships the ball on, and then claps feebly. 'Come on lads,' he calls, just about loud enough for the four of us standing next to him to hear.

'Brilliant as always, lad,' mutters Grub, 'glad I asked.'

Then, in an aside to me that is meant to be overheard: 'It's like being cheered on by a dead sheep!'

Honestly, I wish I had someone else who could catch at second slip. Standing between these two all day can get tiresome.

The next ball beats the bat and slams into Grub's gloves, and he jogs up to the stumps to get a few comments into the batsman's ear. I'm never sure how effective Grub's sledging is if you don't speak broad Newcastle. He comes trotting back to the rest of us.

'Have we got those drinks with the committee after the close?' he asks.

I groan. 'Oh, for fuck's sake.' *I'd forgotten that. Now I feel really depressed.*

'You don't like them?' chirps up Tayls from second slip. 'I don't mind it.'

Grub snorts. 'Oh, we know *you'll* be there. Bit o' free drink and grub. You'll be first there and last to leave. You're the tightest man I've ever met!'

'Oh, here we go . . .'

'Mate, you haven't bought a round in five years.'

'That's bollocks.'

'I've been meaning to ask you actually – in the hotels we stay in, do you collect all the *little* bottles of shampoo from your room, or do you carry a *big* bottle round with you and decant them into it?'

'I have actually got a picture of a beer he bought me once,' I join in. 'I'll always treasure it. It cost him a whole shilling, you know.' The rest of the close fielders chuckle.

He shakes his head. 'Talkin' shit, guys.'

'It wouldn't be so bad,' carries on Grub, 'if you'd ever

been short of money in your life. You can never have too much money to be white trash, eh Tayls?'

'Your family rich, Tayls?' someone asks.

'Yeah, they own this big place up north,' I say. '. . . *Shropshire*, I think it's called.'

'His school had its own zoo!' Grub says incredulously. 'And a golf course.'

'It was only nine holes.'

'Only nine? It was tough in the ghetto, hey Tayls?'

'You can't talk when it comes to schools, though, Mac.'

'No, fair point. Your school not like that then, Grub?'

'No, funnily enough, my school was a bit different. Bit rougher, if I'm honest.' He settles down into his stance as the bowler approaches the wicket. '*We* had our own coroner,' he says out of the corner of his mouth.

The next ball is a beauty. It rears up off a length, takes the shoulder of the bat and spoons to gully. As one man, we are up off the ground, already starting to celebrate as we watch the ball loop through the air towards the waiting fielder.

This is it, we really are back in this! They're going to be 15 for 3.

But then it hits Casey's hands and pops out. It is a regulation chance, a 99-out-of-100 – maybe even more than that – chance. But it doesn't stick. He grabs at it as it bounces away from him, but only grasps air, and the ball lands on the turf at his feet. He stares at it as if he can't understand what just happened.

And just like that, the belief starts to drain out of the team. The energy has been flattened a little, and suddenly the batsmen look more at ease. They get a couple of boundaries away through the field. A moment ago we felt as though we were hunting them; now we are chasing leather. The bowlers are tiring: our moment, our chance, feels as if it has passed us by.

Grub and I are doing our best. Clapping and shouting, encouraging and cajoling, but it feels as if the tide is against us now.

We all drop catches, even the best of us – no one drops them on purpose – and I am careful not to show anything. I am impassive as the cameras focus on me for a reaction. At the end of the over I make sure I jog over to him.

'Bad luck, Case. Don't worry. Keep going.'

Grub finds him and has a word as well. But in my head I am finding it harder to be fair. *It was a dolly. Surely you don't drop those unless you aren't concentrating, or didn't watch the ball, or the pressure's got to you. If he wasn't such a smug, arrogant . . .*

I shake my head.

Come on, Mac. Other things to worry about!

Both opening bowlers are labouring now. I've left them on too long already. We desperately need another over out of each of them.

If they can just grab us another wicket now.

But it is looking less and less likely as they tire.

The next over, from our other opening bowler, is a poor one, with three of the first five balls going for four. And then, as he runs in for the last ball of the over, Ben pulls up short. He stops, stretches his left thigh, his hand holding the back of his leg. He walks back to his mark and sets off again, but pulls up short almost immediately.

He shakes his head and makes a cutting motion across his throat to indicate that he is done.

Fuck! That's all we need.

Maybe it's just a precaution; he knows this is almost certainly his last over of the evening anyway. Caution would be the sensible course with any slight tweaks at this stage. But, my instinct is that it's worse. The way he turned straight towards the pavilion and limped off had a finality about it.

An over later, the ball slides off the face of the bat and runs away towards third man. I turn and give chase. I am flying after it, flat out. But I'm going to catch it, save a run, maybe a couple if the batsman have dawdled a bit.

I'm just about to dive when Casey slides in from the side, nearly flattening me in the process. I have to pull out of the dive and throw myself sideways on to the ground to avoid a collision; my knee twists under me, and a flash of pain arcs up my leg.

Casey fumbles the ball, takes a couple of goes to re-gather it and the batsmen jog back for a comfortable third. I wait for an apology, but he doesn't even look at me, just jogs back into position. *Christ, could this kid act like any more of a dickhead?*

I am doubled over. My knee is in trouble, and I don't trust it to support me yet. I take a couple of steps and the pain jabs at me again. I can just about hobble back to where Grub is looking at me, worried.

'You all right?'

'Not sure.'

'Is that your bad one?'

'Yeah.' This knee has grumbled on for a year or two now. It will, in all likelihood, end my career eventually. The medics have done what they can, but they can only manage it, they can't fix it.

A few overs later, and the knee has got tighter and sorer. It is swollen and tender, and any attempt to move quickly elicits a painful flash of complaint from it.

Grub catches me wincing. 'Go and get that sorted,' he nods at my leg. 'We'll be OK for a bit.'

'I'm all right. Doc can look at it at the close of play.' I look up at the clock, six minutes to go.

'Come on lads. Let's take one with us.'

Friday, close of play

Australia   348 and 54 for 2 (15 overs)
England   179 all out

The doctor's grim-faced examination does not take long. There is no mystery here, and not much to be done about it.

'We'll try and get the inflammation down with icing, and Mark can get into it to maintain your range of motion, but to be honest there's not a huge amount we can do with it, as you know.'

He packs the knee in bags of ice, which he straps in place. 'Twenty minutes.' He starts his stopwatch. There was a time when twenty minutes of icing like this would have been purgatory, but years of undergoing the treatment have almost removed any sensitivity to cold from that leg.

He hands me a couple of paracetamol then leans in closer and lowers his voice, 'I can't give you anything stronger, I'm afraid. Not with your history.' I nod. *No opiates for us addicts, doc, I understand.*

Ben is next to me in the medical room. His news is worse. Torn hamstring, grade 2; out of the rest of the match.

If all you know is cricket, then cricket can break you.

On any given day, my ability as a cricketer is dependent on how well I am able to bat, plus a large slice of luck.

But we are never talking about just one day. A career is not an afternoon. It is not a single moment in time where you have to be good enough.

We are judged on weeks, upon months, upon years, of daily tests. And not on the days when we feel good. But on the ones when we are carrying injuries, when we are ill, when we are out of form and don't know where the next run is coming from; when we are recently bereaved, when we've been on the road for six months, when the kids are sick and we haven't slept for two nights; when we just got hit on the hand in the warm-up and can't feel our fingers. When we're angry, when we're scared, when we're exhausted, and when we're downright sick of the whole charade. That's when we're judged, and how well you can bat is only *part* of it.

The health of your life away from cricket is key to your career within it. We need our back stories, our safe spaces that we can retreat into. The sanity and banality of normal.

You are only as strong and resilient as your hinterland.

If all you know is cricket, then it will break you.

★

Time has many patterns, and flows in different and varied ways. But there are two of these patterns that are pre-eminent in making our lives intelligible and meaningful.

The first is the *arrow*. The arrow of direction that flies forward from cause to effect. It gives our stories stages and causality, beginning-to-end, birth-to-death. The arrow supplies route and meaning to narrative, direction to our lives. We feel its presence intuitively; look for it even when it isn't there. *Post hoc, ergo propter hoc.*

The second defining pattern is the *cycle*, the flowing of time in nested loops of various sizes, endlessly repeating – the cycle of days, weeks, years, and generations. And these ground and stabilise us amid the confusing blizzard of random events. Patterns that repeat: constantly, understandably.

Comforting and stable, they give us the bedrock to construct ourselves and our lives.

Monday morning, Friday night, the weekend, and repeat.

New Year, Valentine's Day, spring, Easter, summer, back to school, Bonfire Night, Christmas, begin again.

The bittersweet cycles of fathers and sons, mothers and daughters. Dad throwing balls to me, and me throwing balls to Sam.

As technology improves, we increasingly find ourselves in a world without time's natural rhythms, either the ones that we forge into stories, or the bittersweet cycles that ground us. The lights come on at 7 a.m. in winter, summer and spring.

But the more the modern world removes or flattens these cycles, with electric lights, central heating, strawberries in January, the more we seek to hold on to them. We cling to their remnants and overlay our own artificial rhythms.

The Test

So Christmas is fir trees and snowflakes, whether you are in Lapland or Cape Town or Delhi.

Arrows and cycles, change and stability. We feel the need for their rhythm, miss them when they aren't there. These are the structures with which we make sense of our chaotic lives.

But not *our* lives. Not *our* world.

I am coming towards the end of my twenty-fifth consecutive summer. I haven't spent a winter in England since I was twenty. Just summers at home and summers away, for nearly thirteen years.

Once you step on to the treadmill of international cricket, time's patterns fracture. The cycle is broken. There are no weekends. Winter never comes. One series runs all but seamlessly into the next.

When this match finishes, we will play the One-Day Series. Then we will pack our bags for Test matches in India. Then a tour of New Zealand. Then off to the West Indies. Three weeks break, then back into the English season. That is our schedule for the next six months. Every day looks the same, feels the same. An endlessly shuffling pack of semi-familiar faces, venues and identikit business hotels. I'll be at home for about twenty days if I'm lucky. For the rest of the time, I will be travelling but not moving. Passing time but not progressing.

It is a comfortable life, and an uncomplicated one. Our needs are catered for, our lives simplified and decluttered, leaving us with one thing to focus on, one job to do. We live in a gilded cage and sing for our suppers.

But it is a life lived only on the surface. The superficial connections that you can make in the few days you are in a certain place, you lose as soon as you move on. It is a life that hollows you out. Your outside is tempered and polished smooth, but your roots atrophy. Your soul's hinterland shrinks and disappears.

You have a home, but you don't live there.

You have family and friends, but you don't see them.

The deep connections, to place and loved ones, and to the normal rhythms of life; the connections that nourish you and ground you. They wither.

Touring brings a weariness that permeates your bones and stays there, as you trudge down an endless trail of airports, hotels and training grounds, year after year.

Two a.m.: you've landed in another strange city, body clock out of whack, standing in the doorway of another hotel room. Unpack tonight? Or in the morning? Or not at all? Just throw the suitcase into the corner and pull out what you need, as and when. Three days later, stuff it all back in and hit the road again.

The road becomes home. Home becomes a foreign town, where you feel out of place and awkward. You watch your children grow up in time-lapse photography.

With each brief break at home there is a roster of friends to catch up with over dinner, or lunch at the weekend. And then 'We must do this again!' *in 18 months' time*, and I'm gone again.

Transient, rootless. Winterless, weekend-less.

And then you go home, and find that the very thing you've longed for most, for months, can within days become too much. The noise and demanding energy of little kids in a confined space, the wrangling over everything, from bedtime to TV to eating up vegetables. Within a week I'm making excuses not to be there at bedtime; the wine is being uncorked earlier and earlier in the evening. I knock off the alarm clock and turn over, let their mother get them up and take them to school: 'Sorry, jet lag, you know how it is.' Within days I step back on to the plane, with a guilty relief. 'Champagne, sir?'

Thanks, don't mind if I do.

Some players embrace it. Accept it and adapt. Grub will never go home. This is his world now. When he finishes playing he'll move straight into coaching or the media. He'll live his whole life in this travelling circus. He can't go home, and he doesn't need to. This is him now.

The rest of us. We cope. It's the price we pay to play.

And we promise ourselves that when it's all over, time will start flowing again. The roots will slowly grow back. We'll make it to the concerts, and the swimming galas, and the family parties. We'll stop being the bastard who always spoils Christmas. We'll take those weeks away with old friends at their place in France.

And the wounds will scab over and heal.

De-iced, I limp from the medical room back to the dressing room, where Jabba is sitting next to my spot, having returned with Grub from the end-of-day press conference. The players who have already showered are changing into their semi-formal number twos – team polo shirts, tailored trousers. *Oh God, I'd forgotten. Still another phase to go in this day from hell.*

'Drinks with the committee,' I sigh to Jabba.

'Ah yes, of course.' He clears his throat '"Old men who never cheated, never doubted, Communicated monthly, sit and stare . . ."'

'Thought you didn't like Betjeman?'

'Oh, everyone likes Betjeman,' he mutters, lifting himself out of his chair with a groan, 'but some of us just don't care to admit it in public.'

My phone beeps, I glance at the screen.

Sorry you had a bad day. Good luck tomorrow, Beth

I smile. Well, that's something at least.

On the second evening of a Test match at Lord's, the MCC committee requires the two teams to attend a drinks reception at the end of the day's play. So we shower, change into our number twos, and troop downstairs to the Committee Room.

Green-blazered attendants circulate with trays of nibbles and drinks. I take a mineral water and steel myself to try and show willing.

I am standing next to a portrait of an old England captain from the nineteenth century. 'Do you think it was simpler in those days? Or do you think it was just different?'

'I don't know that there was any less pressure,' says Jabba, never one to allow you any self-indulgence. 'They used to say England would rather lose a battleship than a Test match—'

'Is that why we've got no battleships left?' Tayls chips in. As always with Tayls, it is hard to tell for certain whether he is being stupid or clever. I give him the benefit of the doubt.

'That's very good for you, Tayls.'

'Thanks . . . and also . . . fuck off, don't be so patronising,' he says with a smile, and wanders off to mingle.

'You know what Keith Miller said about pressure, don't you?'

I do, it's one of Jabba's favourite quotes, and he brings it out whenever he thinks I'm feeling sorry for myself. The great Australian all-rounder flew fighter-bombers during the Second World War. He was later asked about the pressure of playing Test cricket. 'Pressure is a Messerschmitt up your arse . . . Test cricket is fun.' Jabba delivers the line with a passable impression of the great man.

'Nod sush a greyday.'

'I'm sorry?'

A large suit with an even larger man squeezed into it has appeared next to me. He tries again, with the single-minded focus of the very drunk.

'I said, not sush a great day. Fyoo lot.'

Out of the corner of my eye I see our media manager melt away. *Cheers, Jabba.*

'No, we've definitely had better.'

The man lurches forward and I get treated to the full olfactory delight of a day's hard drinking. His broken-veined face is flushed, and fleshy lips work asymmetrically, as if he has had a minor stroke.

'Dizappointingg . . .' he starts. I wait for him to finish, but he leaves it hanging there.

'Yes,' I agree after a while.

'I said "dizappointingg". Dizappointing day . . .'

'Yes.'

'. . . to have to watch.'

'Yes, sorry about that.'

'I hoped yud do bit bedder than that. Give'z bit more to cheer.'

I nod.

'Gotta . . . pitch 'tup a bit.' He thumps my arm. 'Pitch 'tup bit more. Getit swings . . . swingingg.'

Trying to change the subject, I stick out my hand. 'I'm James, by the way.'

'Yes, knew that.' He shakes my hand. 'Call me . . .' but I never find out what to call him because then he spots someone over my shoulder. 'Der'k, Derek, come here a minute.'

He waits.

'Derek.'

I look behind me and find a small, tubby, balding man in deep conversation with Casey.

'Derek! Derek!' Either this isn't Derek, or he is deaf, or he is as drunk as his friend, because even though we are three feet away, he doesn't acknowledge Call Me's shouting.

'Jus' givim a nudgge!' he urges me.

'Err . . .'

'DEREK!' Most heads in the room turn, including the one belonging to the man who may or may not be Derek.

'Cometell . . . Come and tell . . .' He is waving his arms and nodding in my direction. 'Say what you tol' me b'fore.' He nods to me meaningfully. 'Z'gud point!'

'More water, sir?' A tray with a selection of drinks has appeared at my elbow. I swap my empty glass for a fresh one. Derek has joined us. He helps himself to a glass of red and starts pointing at me with it, his bloodshot eyes not quite focused.

'Verr important we win this one,' he drawls. He waves the glass again, and takes two unsteady steps sideways. 'Hope you realise.'

'Yes, well . . .'

'Not just 'nother match . . .' nother day at the office.' He shakes his head and bumps into a passing tray of canapés. 'Key match. Key match.' He is leaning forward for extra emphasis, and his belly, straining at the buttons of his expensive shirt, is bumping against my arm. Call Me is leaning in from the other side.

'Key match,' he echoes, but Derek has got distracted.

'That chap Thomas took a great catch though, didn't he?' He's pointing over my shoulder at Tayls.

'Err, that's not . . . anyway, it was Grub who took the—'

'I'll just go and congratulate him,' and he strides off to shake Tayls by the hand, call him by the wrong name, and congratulate him on a catch he didn't take.

I seize the opportunity to wander off myself, and squeeze myself into a corner next to Jabba. His usually Eeyorish eyes are twinkling, having as usual missed nothing.

'Making friends?'

'Just shoot me now.'

'This'll be you in twenty years' time.'

'Please don't . . .'

'Guardians of The Laws of Cricket. *Laws*, mind, not *rules* like any other game. Presumably they were passed by Parliament or derived from first principles by Newton.'

You can't fight him in this mood, just go with him and enjoy the ride. 'Harks back to a grander age, Jabba, when most of the globe was pink and the penalty for Obstructing the Field was transportation.'

'*Is* there any other institution that more perfectly epitomises why the rest of the world hates us, than the MC-fucking-C?'

Thankfully there isn't time to answer, as the room is being called to order by a large committee member in a tweed jacket. Big-boned, his huge, florid hands twisted with arthritis, he has the look of an ageing second-row forward, one of those men whose bodies seem too big for old age and start to collapse in on themselves. Leaning heavily on his stick throughout, he makes a short speech and a presentation to the Australians. He has a dry sense of humour and speaks well, apart from misremembering the name of the Aussie captain, whose teammates smirk gleefully behind their hands next to him.

I think that might be it for the speeches, but our chief exec steps forward to reply, I assume, on our behalf.

'Look out, Jabba, it's your nemesis,' I whisper.

Grub hears me. 'Diabetes? Where?' he grins.

I don't know if the speech is prepared or off the cuff, but either way it isn't very good. He makes a couple of weak jokes at the Australian team's expense that fall flat, and only succeed in irritating them and making him look petty – *not a complete loss then.*

There is a way of speaking, common to those in power. Headmasters, PMs, CEOs. What Shelley called the 'sneer of cold command'. Maybe it's a brittleness from speaking when you wouldn't choose to, to people who wouldn't choose to listen if they didn't have to. Maybe it's boredom, or staleness; trying to say the same thing to the same people too often. Or maybe they know there's no comeback: speak well, speak badly; no one's going to act any differently towards them. Power assuredly corrupts in many ways.

When he has finished, I try to seize the moment.

'Right then, Jabba, I think we've shown willing. Let's slip out, shall we?'

He downs his drink and ushers me towards the door. 'Let us go then, you and I / When the evening is spread out against the sky . . .

'Like a patient etherised upon a table,' he is reciting increasingly loudly as we leave through the back door. 'Let us go, through certain half-deserted streets / The muttering retreats / Of restless nights in one-night cheap hotels . . .'

'Hardly cheap, Jabba,' but he is already skipping ahead, and intoning:

'There will be time, there will be time / To prepare a face to meet the faces that you meet / There will be time to murder and create / And time for all the works and days of hands / That lift and drop a question on your plate . . .'

'Now you are just showing off,' I tell him.

'In the room the women come and go / Talking of Michelangelo . . .' He is waving his arms around now as he skips to the refrain. 'In the room—'

'Just how many have you had?' I interrupt his flow.

'Alcohol,' he says grandly, 'is both the cause of – and solution to – all my problems.'

'Larkin again?'

'No,' he grins, pleased with himself to have fooled me, 'Homer Simpson.'

'You're as bad as that lot.' That stops him, and I get an accusing look and an affronted silence as we head out into the summer night.

There is a crowd outside at the rear of the pavilion, waiting for autographs, and it is a few minutes before I can turn and head towards my car.

'Mac! Mac!' The voice behind me as I get to the car park is instantly recognisable. I turn to find the familiar face among the crowds. Mark Wyatt was my best friend at university, and best man at my wedding. He catches up with me and we hug.

'Sorry mate! Shit day,' he says, grinning ruefully. 'Time for a drink?'

'Of course,' I grin, 'come on. I'll give you a lift back to our hotel and we'll find somewhere quiet near there. How've you been?'

We find a quiet bar and I pop to the loo. When I return to our small table in the corner, Mark lifts a glass to me. There is an ice bucket on the table with an open bottle in it.

'To James McCall! Captain of England.' He hands me the other champagne glass. 'Congratulations, Mac!'

He doesn't tell me what's in it, and I know without asking. Dom Pérignon, the 1985 vintage. I know he kept three of the bottles from the May Ball, squirrelled them away for just this sort of moment. He lifts his glass, and toasts: '"Bliss was it in that dawn to be alive . . ."'

'". . . but to be young was very heaven".' I complete the line. Lifting my glass and clinking it against his.

He drinks, eyes closing momentarily, savouring the taste, and the memories of a night thirteen years ago.

He looks at me, puzzled. I've frozen, staring at the glass.

When I stopped drinking, I just stopped. I told almost no one, kept both the extent of my problems and my determination to overcome them from all but a few people. Those I saw regularly just got used to the fact that I was never in the mood for a drink, and it went surprisingly uncommented on.

But I've hardly seen Mark at all in that time, and suddenly

77

I realise he doesn't know. The man who for much of my life I would have called my best friend has just opened a ridiculously expensive bottle to celebrate me achieving my lifelong dream.

And not just any bottle.

I know where it came from. I know what it means and so does he.

The smell of her rooms in Cambridge; and windows, high among the roofs, full of clear, blue sky during endless days. Squeezed into a single bed, staring at the cracks on the ceiling. Day. After night. After day. No days have ever seemed so carefree and perfect, before or since.

I can still feel the thrill of pleasure it gave me to see her walking through college, or cycling down Trinity Street. Still remember the sensation of the world lightening around me if I caught sight of her unexpectedly. Or saw her name on a noticeboard list, or even just recognised her bike chained to a railing outside the lecture halls.

Those days, eternally sunlit, live like some alpine meadow in spring, forever high and untroubled in my mind. The summer sun bounced back from great stone crystals of architectural pasts, and I was transformed. I felt invincible and I batted as if I were.

The year before, I'd endured a miserable first season, all careworn twenties and ignoble ducks. And I'd started my second year the same way. Labouring earnestly for the pittance of runs that would keep me (just) in the team.

But in *that* glorious month I made three hundreds. And it changed me for ever. From that moment on, I knew I could do it. I knew I could survive and succeed at that level. I don't know if I would ever have made it as a pro without that almost magical burst of confidence, belief and runs behind me. Before I met Beth, I had a first-class average of 12. A month later, I had three hundreds and a contract with Middlesex.

That summer, that month.

Successful – beyond my wildest hopes – in both love and cricket, and surrounded by the closest, simplest group of friends I would ever have.

There were six of us who wandered down to the river in white tie, and toasted the sunrise with leftover Bollinger from the May Ball. While we lolled on the bank below him, Mark stood on the bridge, quoting the Romantic poets, and extemporising on how *this was it*. Life was *never* going to be this good again.

I'm sure there were boring days, I'm sure I had exams to revise for. There would surely have been days where adolescent worries and uncertainties darkened my thoughts. There must at some point have been rain. But I don't remember it. In my mind, the sun shines for a month, clear, high and untroubled, bouncing from smiling friends, flattering scoreboards and Beth. Beth, all dazzling eyes, dimples and sun-kissed skin, laughing.

★

I look round the pub.

'It's OK, Mac. I've sorted it, they just charged me corkage.' He nods towards the bar, thinking that I am just worried about us turning up with our own bottle.

God it's been a shit day.

My body aches all over. I am weary to my bones. Mark is looking at me expectantly.

The Test

'Cheers!' I say, raise the glass and drink.

★

We always made each other laugh. It was the first and best thing that bound us to more than mutual lust. It thrilled me beyond measure to find someone who always got the joke, and always gave as good in return. Quick, smart, and witty. Eyes constantly twinkling, the dimples only ever a moment away.

And I could make her laugh. A fact I tested to destruction in the early days. It was the mechanism by which I started to realise that *this* really was *it*.

Needless to say, *I* was in from the start. Besotted from before I'd even spoken to her with the girl two years above me, hopelessly cool and beautiful. I never doubted, didn't even need to think about the fact that she was the one and only. My dream girl.

That *she* might feel the *same*. That this might possibly be, beyond all reasonable hope, a two-way thing, slowly started to dawn on me via that shared sense of humour.

From the very first time we spoke, we found each other funny. And everything else, all the other pieces, clicked into place around that cornerstone. That was what made me *start* to dream.

I knew for sure on Midsummer Common in the middle of a November night.

We'd been to a party, both had too much to drink, and then had a blazing row over nothing. Almost the only serious argument we had in the early days. I stormed out, having behaved like an imbecile, but unable to stop myself. Furious at everyone, incensed by the world, I stomped home through the dark rain, knowing I'd wrecked everything, but too proud and too drunk to go back and try to fix it.

Then, halfway across the common, a hand snuck into mine, pulled me to a stop, turned me round. She was standing barefooted in her flimsy party dress, shivering in the freezing drizzle. Wordlessly, she pulled me towards her, tucked her head into my neck and hugged me. Just hugged me. Held me gently, in the silence of the frozen night, until at last she felt the anger drain out of me.

'Let's not,' she murmured into my ear, 'let's not do that.'

Pulling back she stared at me, her face sombre, half hidden by shadows.

'Take me home, Mac,' she sighed finally.

I looked down at her bare feet. She shrugged wearily, 'I'll go get them tomorrow.'

I hung my jacket round her bare shoulders and hoisted her into my arms. As I carried her back to her room, she laid her head against mine. 'Let's not do that again,' she whispered.

'No,' I agreed quietly. 'Let's not.'

'So how are the kids? Are they well?'

'Yeh, they're OK. Emily's at school now.'

'Wow, already! God, they grow so fast.'

We have finished the champagne and have a pint each of London Pride in front of us. I can still see the Mark of thirteen years ago in my mind: shock of blond hair above a face that was invariably grinning; always great company – relaxed, playful, infuriatingly unreliable.

He has aged, even since I last saw him a year or two ago.

The hair is thinner, his face heavier; a roll of fat sits where his neck meets the base of his skull. But, more than that, he looks worn down, half beaten.

He was my best man. I would have been his, but I was picked to tour New Zealand and so missed his wedding.

'Never mind,' said Beth, acerbic but accurate, 'we'll go to the next one.'

I pushed back at her loyally at the time, but she was proven right, as we both knew she would be, when the marriage broke up three years later. Since then Mark has had a string of semi-serious girlfriends who have come and gone without leaving an impression.

The pub is filling up steadily. There are glances in my

direction, which make me uncomfortable. And the fun is going out of the conversation. I am getting stressed and Mark is now pretty drunk: these are clearly not his first drinks of the day.

At the next table along, a wild-eyed scarecrow sits nursing a pint of lager. He has Einstein hair, a Russian army jacket and a large, tatty pair of headphones clamped over his ears. He is humming loudly to himself and drawing circles on the wooden table with the condensation from his glass.

Mark nods at him. 'He's the only sane person in here,' he mutters, going from cheerful to melancholy in a breath. It is a habit of his that was always there, but has become much more pronounced with age.

He sighs deeply, closes his eyes. 'I'm tired, Mac. The whole time I'm tired. Tired ... of ... fucking everything.'

The conversation starts to go wrong, becomes a monologue, a series of his increasingly irrational complaints about his life. Getting more and more uncomfortable, I look down at the table, trace the ridges rising out of the worn wood like fingerprints.

The feeling has been growing on me for a while that people are starting to stare at me. I don't know if it is real or paranoia, but I am getting edgy to the point of panic. *This isn't right. I shouldn't be here. I need to leave.*

Abruptly I stand up, make my excuses – *playing tomorrow and all that, need to get an early night.* I finish the last of my pint and say goodbye. *Great to see you, thanks for coming, must do this again soon, I need to get to bed.*

Need to get to bed. It's a reasonable nod in the direction of what I *should* do, isn't it?

The Test

But I leave the pub and head back to my hotel room like a wine glass falling towards a stone floor.

Whatever I'm thinking, I know what will happen next. I should say *what I will do* next, but that's not how it works.

When you breach a dam, there's only one thing that *can* come next. When you've built a dam from willpower and habit, from carefully constructed routine and bloody-mindedness, and when you've walked the walls of that dam month after month, and stood atop it in the small, lost hours of the morning. When you've watched and listened, and felt the dark waters sloshing back and forth behind it. Then you know. You know, deep down, what will happen when you crack that dam.

It won't be a small leak, easily repaired. It won't be the exception to the rule that you convince yourself it will be. It will be breach: utter collapse, blind drowning and chaos.

I always have the mini-bar emptied whenever I check into a hotel on tour.

Without fail.

No point being a hostage to fortune.

But, with everything going on in the last few days, this one time I forgot.

So it is still there, fully loaded.

One small hurdle fewer between me and oblivion.

Not that it would have saved me anyway.

'Daddy has to go away again, Emily.'

'Where you going, Dada?'

'Australia. Do you remember Australia?'

'On a aeroplane?'

'Yes, sweetheart.'

'Is it a big one or a lil' one?'

'What do you mean, Em?'

'The aeroplane. You gon' go on a big one or a lil' one in the sky?'

'Err, a big one, I think.'

'Coz there's the big ones on the ground that you can climb inside, and there's the lil' ones you see up in the sky.'

'Oh, I see!' I laugh. 'You'd get on well with Tayls, Em.'

'Do the lil' ones have people in too?'

'They do, sweetheart.'

'They must be very small people!'

DAY THREE

We are lying in her room.

High among the roofs, the window open, the summer air drifting in. Pollen and cut grass, sweet as the start of the season.

'What do you think?' She is rubbing lotion into her legs. I am confused, but to be honest, I am happy just lying here watching her.

'It's a free sample. I got it from The Body Shop.'

'Oh, right.'

She stands up and peers down at her legs. Then lifts the oversized T-shirt she is wearing out of the way.

'It's firming lotion.'

'Firming lotion?'

We both stare at her legs. Her slim, elegant, dancer's legs.

Too late, I realise that I am still expected to offer an opinion, and that now the unintended pause has lengthened into a silence. Aware that I now have to say something significantly coherent to justify that silence, I pause for thought, further lengthening the hiatus.

'Oh, you're rubbish,' she says, dropping sideways on to the bed and pulling her T-shirt down to half cover her thighs.

'No, hang on. Let me see . . .'

I stare at her legs – which I have to say I had never at any point considered anything less than perfect; the idea that they might need to be cosmetically enhanced is simply bizarre – and make a show of evaluating their appearance.

'OK. Well your top leg . . .' I say, tilting my head slightly in a show of concentration, 'that definitely looks firmer . . .'

'My top leg?' she queries. She is lying on her right-hand side, looking at her left leg now, trying to see how it differs from its pair underneath.

'Yes. I would say that the lotion has definitely had an effect on your top leg.'

'What about the other one? The bottom one?'

'Well . . . to be honest . . . it's difficult to tell.'

'What do you mean?'

'Well . . . it's so squashed out of shape by the massive weight of the top leg crushing it that I can't really tell!'

'Mac!'

I duck as the pillow skims my head and hits the wall behind me, then reach out and pull her to me.

Saturday 7.55am

Before I am aware of anything else, I feel the twisted knot of shame and dread where my stomach should be. Something is wrong. Something is *very* wrong.

Oh no. Oh fuck no.

Shreds and tatters of memory start to appear. *Oh, Mac. You didn't.*

I don't remember much, but it is enough to wish I could remember less. I screw my eyes tighter shut, push my face further into the pillow; *please God, make it all go away.* My mind tugs gently at the scraps of memory, bringing others bobbing to the surface.

I prise my eyes open. The sun lancing through the window is unnaturally bright; my head explodes with pain. *Mac, you stupid, dumb, shit-for-brains . . . you . . .*

My internal rant runs out of words, lost in the dawning horror.

My eyes focus on the pillow next to me. Beyond it three small bottles stand empty next to the lamp. Kahlúa says the nearest one. *Kahlúa! Fucking Kahlúa!* It would be funny if it wasn't tragic.

I prise my head carefully from the pillow and am rewarded with another detonation of pain. With a dull self-loathing I take in the rest of the room. I'm lying on top of the sheets, fully dressed. Scattered around the room are the drained contents of the mini-bar, which stands open in the corner. I know without checking that it is empty. When I start, I don't stop. I broke the off-switch long ago. There is a room-service tray on the table. And now I dimly remember calling downstairs for more to drink when the mini-bar ran dry.

Gingerly, I lever myself upright. Three quick steps later I'm emptying my guts into the toilet. For what feels like an age I retch into the bowl; dry heaving long after everything has come up. *I have honestly never hated anyone in my life like I hate myself at the moment.*

From my kneeling position over the porcelain I can see right across the room, to my mobile phone crouching like a traitor in the far corner. *Oh God, I phoned Beth.* I half crawl across the room. And, managing to control my stomach for just long enough, I dial into her voicemail – lucky it's still the same code – and delete the rambling message . . . left at 3.48 a.m. *At least I'm sure I got the right one. Thank God for small mercies.*

I stand up, and manage two steps before my stomach rebels. I stagger back to the loo and retch fruitlessly for a further minute.

I look at my watch. *Shit, Shit, Shit. Not much time.* Normally I'd be at the ground by now; I go in early for a hit in the nets before most people get there.

One glance at the mirror is enough to tell me that I look every bit as bad as I feel. My face is grey and puffy, my eyes bloodshot. *For fuck's sake, Mac . . .* but again I run out words. The person staring back at me is devoid of hope.

I can't have *one* drink.

Never been able to.

Never understood people who can.

I love the hit of the first one – slug of gin, pint of beer, glass of wine; the warmth in your belly, the shiver of relaxation trickling down your spine, the tension slipping gently out of you.

Then who doesn't want the second one more than the first? Who can stop at two? Not me, certainly.

And I like being drunk.

I like the feeling; the absence of doubt, in yourself, your opinions, in anything. The nuances your sober mind obsesses over become invisible. Things are simpler, funnier and easier.

I've always liked drinking.

And I've always drunk hard.

Ever since the teenage me first discovered that beer dissolved the anxious awkwardness that plagued him.

And once I was playing cricket for a living, there was always a reason to have a drink: to celebrate a win, to mourn a loss, or just as a reward after a hard day in the field, or because we had a day off tomorrow . . . or because it looked like rain.

And then one day I couldn't remember the last day I hadn't drunk.

I decided to take a couple of days off . . . and couldn't.

I tried to cut back, but couldn't even get my daily units into single figures. The willpower and strength of character that had once defined me were broken. I was fat, depressed, and not batting well. My average was diving steadily towards 40, the watershed between the good and the merely OK.

And then I got breathalysed. I was in a shunt on the dual carriageway. Not even my fault: the car in front braked, and the car behind ran into the back of me. But I was over the limit. Well over.

And . . . I had Sam and a friend of his in the back of the car.

And . . . it was 3.30 in the afternoon.

In the previous twelve months I had been at home for forty-two days, and had not been the best of company for those.

A week later Beth moved out.

*

Lord's is basking under a pristine sky. The morning sun is already bouncing its heat back from the flawless turf. It is *perfect*. Absolutely *perfect*. The greatest stage for this wonderful sport is at its imperious best.

And I am at the very centre of it, in the middle of my own personal hell.

I'm standing in the huddle, talking to a circle of sunglassed faces.

I'm saying words, hearing them come out of my mouth, but seeing no reaction. Dark-lensed eyes reflect back at me impassively, unnervingly. My words are like stones dropping heavily into a dark pond, but producing neither sound nor ripple.

'Things haven't gone the way we'd like so far, and we're in a bit of a hole. But these are the situations where you have the chance to do something really special.

'To achieve something truly great, something really memorable, you need a situation like this. This isn't where we would choose to be, but it's our chance to bowl the spell – or play the innings – that we remember for ever. Let's make it happen.'

Shame is eating away at my insides. *They know. They must be able to tell.* But if they can, they give no sign. I finish talking, the circle claps, breaks up, and we start the warm-up.

It's like acid in your guts, isn't it?

The overwhelming need to hide what I've done is turning my stomach inside out. To our ancestors, ostracism was a *de facto* death sentence. If the tribe rejected you, then you were left to fend for yourself. If you were left to fend for yourself, then sooner or later you would die. If they rejected you, you died alone. And so *shame*, at its heart the belief that we are unlovable, has a corrosive power all of its own. And that hard-wired, destructive fear, born a hundred thousand years ago, has its fist around my insides.

I keep my shades on throughout the team talk and warm-up, take my slip catches, then stand apart watching the rest of the preparations. I feel like death warmed up, but my stomach is settling a little and at least I'm pretty sure no one else has noticed anything untoward.

Then Jabba appears next to me, sweating in the morning sunshine. His rheumy old eyes have been following me since I got to the ground.

'Mac.'

'Morning, Jabba.'

He smiles his twisted smile. 'Did you slip off the wagon maybe?'

I drop my head. *Fuck it, should have known the one person who wouldn't miss it. Can't kid a kidder.*

'I am such a stupid, fucking ...' I still don't have the words.

A heavy arm lands across my shoulders. 'Easy lad,' he says softly. 'Don't start beating yourself up. You know what ... we're *all* broken. We're all broken and pretending we aren't.'

I want to cry.

He taps my chest with his hand. 'No point punishing yourself now. You've got a job to do. That's all that matters for now. Today is another day. All things in moderation, *particularly* moderation.

'Did I ever tell you about the time I nearly drowned myself?'

I wait for the joke, but apparently he's being serious, so I shake my head.

'We were in Cannes for the premiere of one of Brigitte's movies.' His first marriage was to a French actress of some note. 'She was cheating on me; I was drinking pretty heavily. Can't remember which caused which ...' He shrugs equably. '... either way, I've never blamed her.

'Anyway ... we were on a yacht in the bay ... producer had hired it for the launch party. We were fighting. She was screaming at me . . . then, as I was trying to calm her down she just turned her back on me. I snapped and stormed off . . . furious and pretty pissed. I walked straight off the side of the boat.

'I remember bobbing around in the darkness, looking up at the lights on deck, waiting for people to realise. But no one had even noticed.

'I was so angry I refused to call out for help. Ended up having to swim nearly a mile back to shore . . .'

You have to hand it to Jabba, when he tells a story, it's a *story*.

'. . . washed up on the beach in my black tie, like some low-rent Bond.'

I smile. 'What's your point?'

'Do I have to have one?'

'No, but I'm pretty sure you do.'

He holds up his hands in a 'you got me' gesture. 'If you fall off the boat . . . it's OK to call out for help. Halfway back, I didn't think I was going to make it. Of all the idiot ways I nearly died, that was the stupidest . . .'

'Don't worry, Jabba. I'm not in deep water yet.'

'OK, Mac. OK.'

The warm-up goes on. I feel for the bowlers as they try to get their aching limbs moving. They are weary as hell already and ahead of them, in all probability, is a full day in the field.

Jabba and our new physio are looking over to where Casey is chatting to two ex-England players, both here to commentate on the match.

'Let me tell you a story, Michael. The young player comes into the professional game from school,' says Jabba. 'He is, almost certainly, an avid fan and follower of cricket. He has watched the TV, read the press reports, and listened to the commentators throughout his childhood. It's been the sound-track to his development as a player; those media names are giants to him.

'When he enters the international arena, he finds himself among his childhood heroes, many of them already in the press or commentary box. When he meets them it's a thrill, a day he remembers, and – more than most things in the game – he craves their respect. And almost without exception he will, within a few years, hate their guts.'

'Really?'

'Imagine being the worst coach or parent you could be. Overpraise the kids for things beyond their control, and then delight at any misfortune that may befall them. Punish them at random, on a whim. Be unpredictable, except in the inevitability of your temper. Praise the weak, mean and feckless if they are charming; denigrate the virtuous, the generous and the brave if they are not. Look to your own interests and needs, ignore theirs. Pretend luck is skill and vice versa. Invent lies or half-truths that demean them, and announce these to the world; trumpet them from the rooftops.

'How that child would come to feel towards you mirrors almost exactly the dressing room's attitude to the press. A cocktail of vitriol and bitterness mixed with genuine puzzlement, and the long-soured kernel that was their old desire for approval buried somewhere deep down.'

Jabba shakes his head and smiles his twisted smile. 'Then,' he almost groans, 'the player retires. He surveys the employ-ment options open to him, dips a toe in the water here and there, and settles on going into the commentary box. For a year or two he has a foot in both camps. He tries to be fair, to support his friends who are still playing, and not fall out with the younger guys.

'But then he is told in no uncertain terms by his new employers that *this is dull.* That there are only so many times you can say, "Well, obviously he'll be very disappointed with that" and expect people to keep listening. Those instructions from his new paymasters, the comfort of his new life, the dimming of the memories of what it felt like to be on the receiving end, and the genuine frustration felt by any spectator when his side underperforms start to make him more forthright in his views. He becomes more critical, less admitting of nuance or context, more ready to see misfortune as ineptitude and more habitually critical.

'Mix in some genuine envy for those still in the spotlight. The inevitable jealousy the middle-aged man feels for the athlete who is still young, and whom the public still idolise, and eventually the distance between him and the modern game grows too great; the elastic of memory stretches beyond its critical point and snaps. He becomes the very thing he once detested, and the whole shitty cycle is completed.

'It varies from country to country: some are better, some are worse; each has its own flavour. And there are the honourable exceptions who never fully cross over, who manage to stay enthusiastic and convey their love of the game. But they are few and far between. Most fall.'

Jabba wanders away.

I find most ex-players generally talk about the past. Whatever current incident occurs is seen through the prism of their own career. Old grievances surface at the tug of a random sentence looking for an ending. Hang around an ex-player for long enough, and you will quickly hear his stock stories a dozen times apiece. The world-view, particularly when it comes to cricket, has congealed like milk left out in the sun.

The physio looks at me. 'Are they really that bad?'

'No,' I say, 'although they certainly have their moments. But it's useless to take them on. Never pick a fight with someone who buys ink by the barrel.'

I often wonder how Jabba came to hate the press so much. Most media managers do, admittedly, but not with the vehemence that Jabba does. He used to be a journalist, after all – an award-winning one, at that.

He is a mystery. You only get to see what he shows you.

After the warm-up we head to the dressing room. I am walking between Grub and Tayls, trying to hide the fact that my head is pounding and I feel sick as a dog. As we get to the edge of the pitch, Tayls smiles at one of the sponsor's girls he's been flirting with for the last couple of days.

'You still playing shots there?' Grub asks.

'Just being friendly.' But he looks guilty.

'I can tell he's lying,' Grub says to me, 'his lips are moving.' He turns back to our number three. 'Maybe you just don't have what she's looking for . . .' he continues. 'Like a fully functioning brain, for example.'

At first it looks as if she's going to ignore him, but then, just as we are passing, she flicks her hair and grins at him, before turning away, visibly pleased that he's noticed.

'Hey, hey!' Tayls grins triumphantly, 'I've still got it.'

'Aye,' says Grub. 'So much for penicillin, eh?'

'What . . . no, I didn't mean . . . Oh fuck off, Grub,' he says, loudly enough for a couple of the members in the front row to look over, startled. But he is still grinning to himself as we get to the gate.

'Oozes class, doesn't he?' Grub tut-tuts to me.

'Well it's definitely leaking away somewhere,' I agree.

We head up the steps of the pavilion, our spikes clashing on the stone. I walk past a discarded copy of the *Telegraph* lying between two benches. 'Out of His Depth' shouts the headline, above a photo of me looking harassed.

Grub suddenly lights up. 'Hey, did ah tell yuz aboot mah roond on Wednesday?' His accent gets even broader than normal in his excitement.

'No, go on . . .'

'So we were playing the seventeenth. You know it, don't you, par three, over the water, big bunker on the left. We're one hole up. I'm playing last. They've all missed the green, I put my ball on the . . . oops, sorry sir . . .' He steps sideways to make way for an elderly member.

'Sorry, what was I saying?'

'You were playing the seventeenth,' Tayls reminds him.

'Oh aye, so I put me ball on the . . .' He is distracted as he steps aside again for another member just as we get to the dressing-room door. 'I put my ball on the . . . on the . . . erm . . .'

'Tee?' says Tayls.

'Oh, go on then, if you're making one – white, one sugar.' He pushes open the door and holds it for Tayls to go first. 'Ta lad.'

You have to hand it to him. It might be shooting fish in a barrel, but he does it very well.

Saturday, 11.00 a.m.

Australia	348 and 54 for 2 (15 overs)
England	179 all out

We start the day fairly well. But it doesn't take long before we are under the pump.

With no Ben available, I open with spin at one end and rotate the seamers at the other.

When the sun shines, and the wicket is true, Lord's is a fantastic place to bat. The brushed baize outfield gives you full value for your shots, the ball racing away to the boundary, even up the slope.

Lateral movement isn't the be-all and end-all of Test cricket, but it does have a transformative effect on the balance between bat and ball. That is why teams go to such extraordinary lengths to get the ball moving sideways.

For fast bowlers there are two types of movement: swing – when the ball swerves sideways in the air, and seam – when the ball changes direction as it hits the pitch. A ball that doesn't deviate off the straight averages 45 in Test cricket. That is: there will be, on average, 45 runs scored for every wicket that falls. A ball that swings two degrees in the air averages 21. A ball that seams between 1 and 2 degrees off the pitch will take a wicket for every 15 runs it concedes.

These are axioms from which you can quickly and directly derive most aspects of technique and tactics in the match.

With its initial shine and hardness gone, and no overhead conditions to help, this ball is going gun-barrel straight and the Australian batsmen are in their element. Brought up on hard, true pitches where they can trust the bounce, they are devastating in these types of conditions. And, after a watchful start, their batting is starting to take its full toll on our bowlers.

We are desperate to fight, desperate to compete. But we just don't have many punches left to throw. Certainly none that can seriously hurt the Australians in the position they are in. Ben is off the field. Oak is on one leg. His heroics of last night, added to the load from the first innings, have taken a huge amount out of him. There is little help in the wicket for the spinners. And the rest of the team is starting to look just a bit heavy-legged and weary. We were knackered coming into the match, and we've now been in the field for most of it.

This is a resilient team. Full of tough competitors, hardened to this sort of work, but there are only so many times we can go to the well. They don't look as though they have much left to give.

When Casey drops a difficult chance at backward point, there is a collective dropping of heads. It feels as if the wheels are coming off. We start to make uncharacteristic mistakes. Balls are fumbled for no reason. Mid-off dives over a regulation stop and watches the ball roll to the boundary.

Then we get a chance. A top-edged pull flies high into the leg-side. Two fielders converge underneath it. For a moment it looks as if there will be a collision. Then both, sensing the other, pull out at the last moment, and the ball lands on the ground between them.

The crowd groans, the Australian fans hoot with delight. Oak roars at the sky in fury.

Cricket is a sport where details and complexities multiply exponentially when allowed to. The best teams have a lean efficiency in the way they go about their business. With their methodologies simple, decision-making is quick and sure, their movements and preparations well drilled, co-ordinated.

They are performing no fewer actions than an average team, weighing just as many variables, making the same – if not more – decisions and adjustments. But it doesn't look like it, doesn't feel like it when you're in it. Roles are clear and understood; players and coaches go about their business, focus on their own areas of responsibility and trust those around them to do the same.

From the outside it looks easy and assured, the players and tactics shown off in their best light. Other teams copy the tactics, and pick similar players, often without managing to reproduce the same success.

In lesser teams, by contrast, the same – if not more – effort is being applied, but much of it is wasted; dissipated through duplication of effort and disagreements over issues large and trivial, negated by changes of heart and decisions reversed.

Focus and effort become more internal; less of it is directed outwards towards the team's goals.

More of the details are overlooked or fudged. Boat speed dribbles away unnoticed and unremarked-upon.

The differences are subtle. The margins are small.

The margins between the good and the poor,

the confident and the frazzled,

the half-chances not chanced,

the loose balls watched pass,

the yorker or bouncer not tried,

the nerve not held through the tough patches,

the focus not kept, just when you've inched your nose in front.

The margins are so small as to be largely invisible.

Sometimes, though, you see something that shows you where a team is; a small window into its soul opens. It might be its fielding when under pressure, or its timidity when faced with a small chase.

Today feels like one of those moments.

We are terrible.

Saturday, 1.08 p.m.

Australia   348 and 152 for 2 (44 overs)
England   179 all out

We are slumped in our seats during the lunch interval. The room is quiet, sombre even.

'Anyone seen Reg?' I ask. This elicits only snorts and expressions of disbelief from the room.

'Who?'

'You'll be lucky.'

'Seen him once all week.'

The dressing-room attendant is in charge of keeping everything running smoothly. Everything from restocking drinks and food, to arranging players' laundry and getting things signed by the team. It is one of those jobs that – when done well – you barely notice, but done badly creates mayhem. Most of the roomies are excellent. Reg is useless.

'Honestly, how did they end up with a roomie so rubbish, here of all places?' Grub asks me.

'They actually tried to sack him after he'd been here a year . . .' I say.

'Did they?'

'Yeah, but they couldn't find him.'

Grub snorts in acknowledgement of the joke.

'He makes a point of never looking out of the window in the morning, you know.'

'Why?'

'Because he'd have nothing to do in the afternoon.'

'What happened to Steve?' Oak asks from the other side of the room. Reg had a short-lived assistant who had been a vast improvement. 'He was much better.'

'They got rid of him,' I say. 'He worked too hard. He was making people look bad.'

Next to me Grub is staring at Taylor's calf. 'What have they written on your leg?'

'It's not writing, Grub. It's a tattoo.'

'OK, what have you got tattooed on your leg? It looks like *Fuck.*'

'It's not Fuck, it's Arabic. It's like Kanye's.'

'Kanye?'

'Yeah, Kanye *West.*'

'That's a service station on the M1, isn't it?' mumbles Jabba as he lumbers past. 'Just south of Northampton.'

'How do you know?' Tayls asks him. 'You can't drive.'

'I *can* drive,' he retorts, 'I just *don't.*'

'. . . I'm pretty sure Kanye doesn't have *Fuck* tattooed on his leg, Tayls.' Grub isn't letting it go.

Now that he says it, it definitely does look like he has *Fuck* written on his calf.

'It's not *Fuck*, it's Arabic.'

'What does it mean?'

'I dunno.'

'You don't *know*?'

'They showed me a few and I picked the one I liked the look of.'

'You picked the one that looked exactly like *Fuck*?'

'F . . . Sod off, Grub.'

'Yeah, Grub,' I shout, 'Arabic off and leave him alone.'

'You know the problem with Tayls,' sighs Grub, leaning over, 'is he's not even smart enough to realise he's dumb . . . he's like a cross between a prep-school blazer and a head injury.'

'Look, it was just more simple . . .' Tayls is still trying to justify his selection method.

'There's a word for "more simple",' deadpans Grub. 'It's simpler.'

'What is?'

Grub looks at me despairingly.

I shake my head. 'Don't look at me. You deserve each other.'

Grub gives me his hurt face.

'What can I say?' I tell him. 'You're punching a blind man.'

After a moment, I decide to take it further. 'Why do you get into him so much?'

'Deserves it,' he mutters without looking up. I think that's all I'm going to get, but then he realises I want an answer and tries to frame one. He drops into his seat and looks up at me.

'Why be greedy when you've got more than you could possibly need? It's just being a prick. And I know he feels like he never gets the credit he deserves, but it's fucking hard to give someone due credit when they snatch it for themselves every chance they get, isn't it?'

I nod, and bend to adjust my bootlaces. 'Just go easy, eh?'

He grunts and walks off towards the loos. I glance across to Jabba; he knows what I'm asking him.

'It is always important to remember that just because two people disagree doesn't mean one of them is right,' rumbles the big man.

Vintage Jabba, this. It is rarely one thing or the other. It is rarely black and white. The world consists for the most part of sliding scales.

It is not volume or intensity, it is not nature or nurture, it is not art or science. It's both. The truth is in the balance, the devil in the details.

Gut-shot.

There is a type of Test where you effectively lose the match on day two, but then take three days to bleed out. Gut-shot. Like a cowboy in an old Western.

It goes like this.

First you bowl for a day and a bit. Then you get bowled out, still well behind the opposition total. Now all the dynamics of the game are working against you. Your bowlers are going back into the field without a night's rest. Particularly for a seam-based attack, this means they are nowhere near as effective as they are when fresh. And the longer the third innings goes on, the more tired they get. Their chances of turning the game for you in that state are minimal.

Seam bowlers cover about 25 kilometres in a full day's play in a Test match. Much of that is at a near sprint as they run in to bowl, and that doesn't include warm-ups and everything else they do on a match day. They also have over a hundred near maximal efforts as they bowl the ball. In baseball, a pitcher will be pulled out of the game at around a hundred pitches, and it is generally accepted that he will need four days' rest to recover before he can play again.

The Test

The bowlers have to do all that, and if they haven't bowled the opposition out, they have to get up the following day and do it all over again. *No wonder they're always grumpy.*

Which, when you've been gut-shot, makes it far easier for the opposition batsmen to build up their lead. Once they are well ahead, they are fairly safe. There is little pressure on them, and they are in no great hurry. There is plenty of time left in the match so they can be patient in building an impregnable position. And the longer they keep our batsmen out in the field, the more they sap their legs so that, when they eventually declare or are bowled out, the top order has to face their rested bowling attack with legs heavy and reactions dulled.

The rest is grimly inevitable.

It is what happened to us in the previous Test at Headingley, and is well on its way to happening again.

Daddy?

Sam?

Are you going to come home, Daddy? Are we going to move back to the old house?

I will, Sam, I will. Just not yet.

When, Daddy? Will it be next week?

No, I don't think by next week.

He looks sulky.

I don't understand, Daddy.

I feel as if my chest is splitting open.

I know, Sam. It's hard.

I hug him to me.

It's very hard on you. And it's not your fault.

I can feel his tears on my skin.

He's eight years old now. In eight or ten years my job will be mostly done. He'll be his own person, setting off into the world, and I'll be shuffling into the wings to watch from the semi-distance. The thought of it makes my stomach fall away, as if I've nearly stepped off a cliff.

I think of how much of me now is the influence of Mum and Dad when I was that age. Of how much of the good in me is from them. Already, there are too many sports days and school plays where I arrive just before the end, rush through the doors just in time to hear the applause and see the lights go down on smiling faces.

After Beth moves back to her parents' place with the kids, I stay in our house for a month or so. But eventually their absence drives me away.

The day is fractured by finding the smell of her, for a moment, on a towel. I can't face their clothes, folded on a chair. I walk into another unchanged room. The TV remote, Tuesday's paper, yesterday afternoon's beer cans, scattered.

Radio that I dislike fills the house day and night because I can't bear silence. I crawl into her, unslept-in, half of our bed, hug the duvet too tight.

My drinking is out of control. I wake in the afternoon and stare at the wall. Walk from room to room without purpose. Or take a bottle into the kids' room and weep in silence.

Here is a type of pain from childhood. You can partially defend yourself against most of the blows that come in adulthood, see them coming; throw an arm out to deflect them, or flinch away and roll with the punch. It hits you. Hurts you. But you can deflect some of the force. Avoid serious injury.

This, though. This is the grief you feel as a child. The sort that you don't see coming, that hits you square in the face: un-managed, un-softened pain. Raw, back of the throat: incomprehensible, and impossible to bear.

Just to add a little more hurt into the mix, I get a call from the selectors. England have finally lost faith in me and I've been left out of the winter touring squad. I'm too numb for it to hurt properly.

We had been so happy to find that house. It is perfect, the garden backing on to the river, the hills beyond. It is in the next village over from my parents; we could walk there across the fields for Sunday lunch.

Then one morning I wake on the bathroom floor with no idea of how I got there. Where the memory of last night should be, there is nothing, blackness. I search further; the whole of yesterday is gone. I've no idea what I did, or where I was. My right hand is covered in dried blood. When I soak it in the sink I find a half-healed gash across the palm.

The walls are pressing in on me. I'm finding it hard to breathe.

Needing to get out of the house, I fill a water bottle from the sink and head out of the back door. I gaze round the garden, then find myself following my feet to the path beside the river and setting off.

There is no plan or purpose to the walk, but I feel better for it. The wind on my face is the first thing like pleasure that I have felt in a while, that has not come from a bottle.

After an hour, I come to the point where I normally turn and head home.

But I don't want to go back.

I carry on.

I don't know where the path goes from here. I follow it anyway.

The autumn day is bright and fresh, the sun is warm on my back, and I sweat from the effort whenever I am sheltered from the wind. The river is wider and calmer here, barely moving between its thick, grass banks.

On I plod, hours pass, the miles add up.

My mind is whirring, straining like an overwound mechanism; baffled, and miserable. As close to insanity as I've ever been, unable to make sense of anything.

In the absence of any idea more coherent, I just keep walking.

Darkness falls.

I'm lost, I'm cold, but I keep going, keep putting one foot in front of the other, on into the night. I don't know where I'm going, but I know what I'm leaving behind. By chance I've stumbled on the only plan that makes any sense. Walk away. Just walk away from everything.

Then, ahead, I see the lights of a pub.

I steal myself to walk past it, I'm done with drink. I know that, at least. But the next moment I am stepping through the doors into the waiting warmth. Go on then, just the one – *like hell one.*

As I step up to the bar, I put my hand in my pocket, and realise I don't have a penny on me. The girl behind the bar is looking at me expectantly. 'Sorry,' I mumble, turn, and head back outside.

Saved by insolvency.

I watch dawn rise over a section of dual carriageway I don't recognise.

I beg water from a petrol station to refill my bottle and head onwards.

My feet are swollen and sore, both heels badly blistered, my legs ache, and my stomach is howling with hunger.

But that's OK. Pain is good. Pain is catharsis now.

I press on, into my second day of walking.

The sun is warm, but I am shivering, as well as sweating. I know I can't keep going, but I don't want to stop. Don't want to go back.

Eventually, my body starts to shut down. My legs fold under me without warning, and I sit down hard on the concrete. My mind is snapped out of its hallucinatory fug. And even in my befuddled state, I realise I can't go any further.

In the end, I make the only call I can.

Holding the borrowed mobile to my ear, I listen to it ring, and then to my relief it is picked up, and a familiar voice answers.

'Hi Stocksy,' I say, 'can you come and pick me up?'

Sweating and shaking, I sit there, staring at the door. We both know I'd have been through it hours ago if he weren't still here.

My guts churn. I think I'm going to retch again. I close my eyes and take deep breaths. It helps but, after a minute or two, the insects come back, creeping over my arms and back. I have to open my eyes again to drive them away. I scrub at the skin on the back of my hands, trying to scrape off the feeling of crawling.

He comes back from the kitchen, hands me a fresh mug, and takes his own to the armchair in the corner. I lean forward, plant my elbows on my knees to stop them shaking, cradle the heat of the tea in my hands.

'Any better?'

I shake my head, and regret it as the room tilts and my stomach lurches.

The Test

'Any worse?'

'No,' I swallow, my mouth dust-dry. 'No worse.'

'Drink if you can.' I take a sip. Hot and very sweet, it helps a little. 'If it gets any worse, we'll get you help. You're safe for now, I think.'

He talks slowly, with long pauses for my churning mind to make sense of what he's saying. He repeats himself until he thinks I've got it.

'You can't think your way out of this, Mac. Not even you. Your mind can only confuse you now.' His voice is steady, sympathetic. 'Just get through today. Tomorrow will take care of itself. There is no magic pill, no silver bullet. There is no trick, no puzzle you can solve that's going to fix this quickly.'

He seems to know what I'm thinking. Heads off my racing thoughts each time they start to run wild.

'Your mind got you into this. And it can't get you out of it. You know what you have to do.' Carefully, I lie down on the sofa, thinking it will help. It makes it worse, my guts rebel, and I hurriedly lever myself up again. 'Don't think, don't reason, just keep doing the next right thing. Sit tight. Get through it.'

This is killing me. I need a drink. I can stop again tomorrow when I'm feeling better.

'Wounds heal with time, not with prodding. All you can do for now is to not make it worse.

'Get through the day, Mac. This will pass, it will get better.'

He keeps talking, all afternoon. Stories from his career, from his life before I knew him, but each of them is terrible, the worst situations he found himself in, the worst things he ever did. Slow, simple, and matter of fact, he lays himself bare. He seems to spare himself nothing, allows himself no vestige of pride or dignity.

And it dawns on me what he is doing.

He's climbing down into the hole next to me.

A few days later he drops me off at home. I work my way round the house and empty every last bottle down the sink.

Then I look around and realise it's not enough. I can't stand it here any longer.

I lock the place up and leave it to their ghosts. I find a small flat, move a couple of bags of my stuff in, and manage to stay off the booze.

Saturday, 4.46 p.m.

Australia	348 and 313 for 3 (84 overs)
England	179 all out

The ball stays down and bounces awkwardly just in front of Grub, but as always it melts into his gloves nonetheless. He rolls smoothly, bounces back to his feet and flicks the ball to Casey at backward point. He walks back towards me.

'So how's my godson doin'?'

'He's well I think. You know Sam, doesn't give much away. Not showing any obvious signs of your malign influence yet, at any rate.'

'Don't worry, I haven't really got started yet,' he grins lopsidedly. 'He needs to be a bit older before what I know is useful to him.'

He settles down into one of the 500-plus deep knee bends he does in a day. The next ball comes flying straight through to him, he pops it to me, and I pass it on.

'Err, who's next, Mac?' Grub says it hesitantly, asking the question that someone has to ask. I've been watching this moment slowly approaching for the last couple of hours, praying for some sort of miracle to avoid it.

We are a bowler down. More than that really: Rob has been our fifth bowler all summer, sending down five or six

121

overs of his left-arm spin per day. Without him or Ben to share the load, I have had to bowl the others into the ground. Our off-spinner has been on unchanged from the Nursery End all day, and the seamers have had two long spells each from the other. Now Oak is off the field being treated, and our third seamer looks ready to drop. Our physio found me at tea to whisper darkly into my ear. 'Oakley's done. His knee is in a terrible state. I've told him he mustn't go back out.'

Grub is waiting for an answer.

I shrug. 'Any ideas?'

'Might be time for *you* to roll back the years,' he says grimly.

The same thought had occurred to me. It is a desperate one at that. Early in my career I bowled occasional medium pace. But I haven't turned my arm over in years, not even in the nets.

'Oh God.'

'Do you bowl, Mac?' asks Tayls.

'Bowl? He's got Test wickets!' Grub grins.

'Really, how many?'

'Well I wouldn't . . .' I start to say.

'Six.'

'You've got six Test wickets?'

'I think it would be more accurate to say that I happened to be bowling while six batsmen managed to get out.'

And so it happens.

Like someone trapped in a bad dream, I take off my sweater and hand it to the umpire. I start to pace out my run-up. *Christ, I'm not even sure I can remember how many strides it's supposed to be.*

I organise the field, bowl a few balls to mid-off and, when I can delay it no longer, I walk to my mark, turn and set off.

The first ball is so slow that the batsman is almost undone by its lack of pace, and plays three different shots before it gets to him. He very nearly ends up chipping it to mid-on.

Oh God that hurt!

The unfamiliar movement has nearly snapped my shoulder and back. My knee sends out a scream of complaint. I wince, stretch and set off back to my mark. The rest of the over doesn't go too terribly. The gentle pace is throwing out the batsman's timing and he is being ridiculously watchful, treating each ball like a potential hand grenade. Even though it could, in all honesty, be played quite comfortably with a stick of rhubarb by one of Geoff Boycott's female relatives.

My second over isn't treated so charitably, and I get smashed to the boundary three times. My third over is worse. The crowd is getting restless, and I can't blame them for a second.

Exasperated shouts bounce from the stands.

'Come on England!!'

'Get someone else on!'

'What are you *doing*?'

'Keep going, mate,' Grub says quietly as we get ready for the next over.

'How's it hitting the gloves?' I ask ironically.

'I'll let you know when one gets to me,' he mutters back with a half-smile.

There is a delay for some reason, the umpire is holding up play. The twelfth man is running off the pitch. I look over my shoulder, puzzled.

Down the steps and on to the field limps The Oak. The crowd aren't the only ones unhappy with what they've been watching, it seems.

He can barely force his body into a jog as he hobbles over to us.

'Maybe I should take the next over at your end?' he says with a sad smile.

I look down at his leg. 'You sure?'

He looks down too, and then shrugs. 'Don't think I can make it any worse now, to be honest.'

'Thanks, Oak.'

At the end of the over, the batsmen take a drink and get fresh gloves. I take the opportunity to get the whole team into a huddle.

'OK, listen. We know we've not been good enough out here today. And it's fair to say that we're not in a great place in the match.

'But, if there's one thing about being in a shit position, it's this. No matter how bad things get, you can always make it better, and you can always make it worse. Those fuckers up there are watching us. Waiting for us to crack. Looking for the moment that they think we've given up.

'So, for the next hour, each of us takes responsibility for ourselves, and our own standards. The bowlers are going to set the tone, and we're going to back them up.

'The next hour matters. It matters how we end this innings. It matters that we keep fighting, keep making it as hard for them as we can.

'There's weather around for the next two days, this wicket is still flat. This match isn't over, unless we give up now.'

★

And in he comes. Crippled knee be damned, he charges in ball after ball. It doesn't materially improve our dreadful position in the match, but it does at least look like a Test match now.

Oak is doing this for pride alone. And it is magnificent to watch. I don't care what anyone else thinks.

I can almost see Jabba at the back of the Press Box, rheumy eyes looking up from his iPhone, intoning under his breath.

Now the sunset's breezes shiver,
And she's fading down the river,
But in England's song for ever . . .

Last Monday afternoon

On the way down from Headingley to Lord's, I go home to see Dad. It's only five miles out of my way, and I haven't seen the old fella for a month. I call him from the car, but get no answer. I see why as I roll down the long tree-lined drive at the front of school, and park up.

As I round the red brick of the boarding houses, I can see him in the nets. He is giving throw-downs to one of the younger kids. The movements are a little stiffer, less fluid, but the arm is still strong – the rhythm of the practice hasn't changed. I could see it precisely with my eyes closed – back to his mark, wheels round and sets himself, feet apart, three steps gathering pace and then the long fluid throw, arm high. The follow-through I don't know so well. I was always watching the ball by then.

The boy is tiny, dwarfed by his kit. The helmet wobbles on his head, the pads force his gait into a waddle. He looks like a typical project for Dad. 'The little ones always learn best' is one of his maxims. In the lower years at school, the game is still dominated by the boys who've grown early, the ones with the size and strength to smash the ball to the boundary.

The Test

A small boy – even one with the ability and temperament to partly compensate for his size – has to fight far harder, be much better technically, just to get in the side. These are the ones Dad will pour hours into, honing their skills so that in a couple of years when they grow into their strength, they seem to emerge, fully formed, as the finished article.

He never coached a team I was in. As I came up through the school, he dropped down from the 1st XI to the U14s just as I was about to join the senior squad. There were plausible reasons given at the time, but he was keeping his distance, keeping the roles simple and clear.

That's not to say he didn't coach me. He threw thousands of balls at me in our own time. During the holidays, in particular, we would be in the school nets most evenings. I would have to drag him out there, plead with him to come and play while he moaned about his sore shoulder or all the jobs he had to get through. It was a charade, of course, he enjoyed our daily hits as much as I did, but he always made me take the initiative, made me drive it. It was his little safety net to stop him turning into *that* parent.

Each night there would be a different challenge: to hit the second pole twice in a row with off-drives, or to survive for twenty balls with him bowling at me properly; or imagined match scenarios where I would try to guide my side to victory in the closing overs of a run chase. He was and is a brilliant coach, and every long summer evening was a delight.

Not every night. I was a sports-mad kid and the school was my playground. Some days I'd swim, sometimes there'd be endless grudge matches to play against my older sister on the tennis courts. Other days I'd be over at friends or playing football in the park. But most days my kit bag would catch my eye at some point, and the negotiations would start. Three hours later we'd be squeezing one last over into the dying light, an exasperated Mum keeping supper warm at home.

When I made my Test debut, he appeared in Sri Lanka. Knocked on my hotel-room door the day after I phoned him to tell him I was playing. And he was there for every innings he could be in the years that followed.

Not now though.

He doesn't watch me any more.

Not since Mum died.

'Marcus, this is my son James, say hello.'

I reach out to shake his hand.

'Hi Marcus, pleased to meet you. How's it going?'

The little boy's eyes are like saucers. He mumbles something unintelligible.

'Not working you too hard, is he?'

The boy shakes his head solemnly.

'Good.'

'Tell you what, Jim, you go and put the kettle on,' says Dad, putting the lad out of his misery, 'we're just about done here. You know where it is, don't you?' I nod; he throws me his keys and starts picking up the balls.

It's the first time I've seen the new place. It suits him. Suits who he is now. Neat, self-contained, tucked away in a corner of the village, a small garden backing on to the river.

We sit looking out from his study. It's a fine August day and the sun streams in through a large bay window.

'This is where I write, meditate and — ' he nods to the window – 'watch the river.'

'Does it do much?' I ask cheekily.

'No . . . but that's why I like watching it.'

We lapse into silence.

'How was the move?'

He makes a wounded gesture, half shrug, half flinch, to indicate the incomprehensible pain of it all. We sit quietly for a while.

'How's the writing?'

Dad sighs. 'Good and bad.

'I don't know . . .' He looks out of the window for a minute, trying to frame his next thought. 'I think I wish I'd *done* more.

'I sometimes think the danger of *teaching* is that you end up being in the world but not of it. You live too much of your life vicariously. It's not supposed to be about you. You are supposed to do the work, set everything up, organise, coach and encourage, and then stand applauding from just offstage. Your whole focus is on others' achievements. It's a habit that becomes engrained if you're not careful. You feel old too early, and accept it.'

I laugh. 'If you want to feel old early, try my job!'

He smiles, but continues. 'I sometimes wonder whether to write well about the world you have to be in it, and that maybe I'm not.'

The river burbles at the end of the garden.

'Last year, do you think?' I ask.

He looks at me, pauses, and then nods.

As he has got older, he's picked up certain mannerisms.

He's started to quibble. He corrects people when he doesn't need to; overemphasises simple points pedantically. It grates on me, and I'm unfairly snappy with him about it. The truth is that it really burns me when he does it, and I know exactly why.

I don't like seeing weaknesses in him, weaknesses he used not to show. But my reaction goes beyond that, and the reason I'm so particularly sensitive to it is because I'm seeing faults I know in myself. Seeing him do the things I work hard to stop myself from doing. It's a restraint I learned from him, and always admired. So when I see him doing it, it feels as though he isn't trying. And so, entirely unfairly, I find myself taking his decline personally.

I tried to talk it through with Grub. But he just looked at me blankly. His relationship with his father was very different. 'T'be honest, Mac, we didn't really get on. When I ran away from home, my dad sent me a message saying, "Don't come home, and all will be forgiven".'

However my career goes, it is likely that, give or take a year, Dad and I will retire at the same time. A strange thing to happen, that.

'For he who lives more lives than one, more deaths than one must die', Wilde says in *The Ballad of Reading Gaol*. Retired cricketers understand him well. The end of their career, and the life it gave meaning to, comes too soon and too fast for many. That death and rebirth is the making of some of us, the breaking of others, but changes us all.

When you leave the dressing room, where you've lived the best moments of your life, you step out into the world, and a silent door locks behind you that never reopens. However many friends you have in the room, you've crossed a Rubicon.

The thing you did first and foremost. The thing that defined you, even to yourself, is gone. *For ever.* The central pillar of your identity and self-worth disappears. How stable a person, how rounded an individual do you have to be to take that in your stride and not stumble?

It is a very balanced man who is unaffected, who isn't disturbed by the shifting ground beneath his feet.

Out into the world you go, with your career stats and

your memories. With your bitterness at injustices, real or imagined. And your envy towards those still in the light, who still get to play, who still have the warmth of the dressing room around them, and who the girls' eyes still follow.

Saturday 5.41pm

Australia   348 all out and 405 for 7 dec (105 overs)
England   179 all out

We just about hold it together. We pick up some wickets to at least slow their progress, but they are still able to declare before the close in a near impregnable position, leaving us an awkward last half-hour to negotiate.

When we get off the field, I go straight to the medical room, get my knee strapped in ice, then hobble back to the dressing room. Blazered members stare at me as I limp along the corridor, the bulging bags strapped to my leg. One holds the door open in silence, sniffs disapprovingly, then turns his back. *OK, mate, it's not exactly the day I had in mind either.*

Stepping through the door, I almost run headlong into the chief exec, who is bustling hurriedly the other way.

'Well then,' he says severely, 'not great, eh?'

'No . . .'

'Not what we'd hoped for exactly.'

I shake my head.

'Have you seen Jabba around?'

I shrug. 'You tried the Press Box?'

'Yes. Not there. Well, if you see the fat incompetent, tell

him I need to speak to him.' And he turns his back and walks away.

Well, fuck you too.

I totter painfully into the dressing room and head towards the balcony. Applause ripples round the ground, as our openers walk out to the middle.

'What's up with Tayls?' someone asks behind me. I turn round to see most of the room staring at our number three batsman, who seems to be having trouble doing up his pads. He looks groggy; something clearly isn't right.

'Get the doc,' I say, crossing over to him. He looks up at me, his eyes struggling to focus. 'A feel a bi' wooozy,' he slurs. He looks as if he's had ten pints. His eyes keep drooping shut and then opening again.

Grub is at my shoulder, 'Did he take a knock to the head, like?'

I shrug, 'I don't remember him doing.'

Doc rushes in and takes control.

'How are you feeling, Tayls? Can you talk to me?' He lifts an eyelid and examines his pupil; his other hand is on his wrist, feeling his pulse. 'He's taken something,' he says, almost to himself.

'What did you take, Tayls?'

Tayls shrugs. 'Jus' th'usual,' he slurs, waving his hand at the seat beside him. There is an empty pill packet sitting there.

'He has got hay fever,' says the doc. 'He always takes antihistamines before he bats.'

I hand him the empty packet. He reads the back and groans. 'Did you take these, Tayls? Is this the packet you took?' Tayls is now barely conscious. I reach forward and shake him. He blinks blearily, not particularly aware of where he is. 'How many did you take? Tayls, how many did you take?'

He holds up two fingers, 'Twooo . . . Reggie got them f'me.'

Doc sighs. 'These are the sleeping pills I gave him a couple of days ago. The genius has taken the wrong pills. Two won't be dangerous, he's just going to be unconscious for the next fifteen hours or so.'

'Sleeping pills. You fucking numpty!' Grub yells at him, punching him hard on the shoulder.

'Hey, liv' 'lone,' mumbles Tayls without opening his eyes, and is sound asleep again within moments.

This is a horrible time to bat. Tired legs, tired minds from a whole day in the field. Your reactions are necessarily slowed a little, your reflexes dampened. The next forty minutes could be critical to us having a chance of saving the match. It is the sort of situation that Tayls is perfect for. Solid, seemingly nerveless, he absorbs pressure and brings a sense of calm and security to proceedings. I look down at him snoring in his chair and want to punch him as well. *Numpty is right.*

I look up at Casey. He is padded up ready to go in at four. It's a huge ask to push him up the order in this situation. Like everyone else, he looks tired and edgy. I look round the room. There is no one else. *Only one thing for it, Mac.* I make my decision.

'You stay four, CT. I'll go three. Everyone else shuffle up one until the village idiot here wakes up.'

I bend down, rip the ice bags off my knee, cross to my place and start getting ready. There is a howl from the pitch followed by the roar of a wicket. *Shit.* I look up at the screen:

LBW. The dismissed batsman walks down the wicket, talks to his partner, then reviews the decision. *Well, that at least gives me a chance of being ready in time.*

Whatever hope he had that made him review the call is quickly proved wrong, and Hawk-Eye confirms the Out decision. By then, I am ready. I pick up my bat and head out of the door.

Saturday 6.19 p.m.

Australia	348 and 405 for 7 dec (105 overs)
England	179 and 11 for 2 (5.3 overs)

My efforts to protect Casey are short-lived.

Soon after I get to the crease, our other opening batsman is caught second slip, and Thomas walks out to the middle. We still have a difficult two and a half overs to negotiate before the cut-off time at the end of the day.

His first two balls are absolute jaffas. One angles in towards the stumps and then jags away, beating the outside edge of his bat. There's a chorus of *oohs* from the close fielders and a snarl from the bowler. The next goes the other way, bouncing and nipping back; it misses the padding and slams into the flesh of his thigh. There's half an appeal from behind the stumps but the ball is clearly going over. The bowler follows through to within a couple of yards of Casey, snarling and glaring. The youngster stares back, unmoved. He refuses to break eye contact and for a moment there is an impasse, but eventually the bowler spits and turns away to walk back to his mark.

Casey settles back into his stance and the bowler charges in again. The next ball is a fraction too full and the debutant slams it back past the bowler for four, the full face of the bat flowing elegantly, straight through the line of the ball.

Every now and again a shot is so crisp, so clean, so apparently effortless, that it takes your breath away. The balance, the timing, the precision required, with a ball travelling at 90 mph. The split second the ball is in the air just doesn't seem long enough. It's almost as if batsman and bowler have choreographed the moment together, the only possible way to arrive at such perfection. The ground gasps and then roars its approval.

Wow, this kid can PLAY.

The last few minutes of play pass uneventfully, and Casey and I troop back to the pavilion, past the high-fiving Aussies celebrating a spectacular day for the tourists.

I slump into a corner and start taking my pads off.

'Err, Mac?' Jabba has lumbered up to my chair.

'What is it, Jabba?'

'Err . . .' He has that look on his face again.

'Come on then, spit it out. What have you got for me, Jabba?' *Sometimes he is just too much.* At the moment I really don't need any witty *bons mots* from our very own Oscar-fucking-Wilde.

He doesn't say anything

I snap, rounding on him angrily, 'Come on, Jabba!' I hiss at him under my breath. 'I feel like shit, as you already know. We are five hundred runs behind and two down already. There are two days left and the weather forecast is improving by the minute, so barring a freak accident, or an airstrike, the Ashes are heading south for the winter.' I'm aware that I'm getting louder and louder, but I can't stop myself.

'Our dressing room looks like A&E on a rough night and our number three has anaesthetised himself and is likely to be unconscious till Christmas because . . .' I'm momentarily lost for words. '. . . because he's a fucking simpleton!' I have slowly crescendoed to a shout by the end of my rant.

'Steady on,' someone says.

'What?' I round on them. 'It's not like he can hear me, is it?' I jab my finger in the direction of Tayls, who is snoring loudly in the corner.

'He's in danger of giving imbeciles a bad name . . . So come on, Jabba, *what have you got for me?*'

For a moment I don't think he's going to answer, but then:

'Who's going to do the press?' he says at last, with a look that suggests he would rather be anywhere on earth but here saying this.

I open my mouth and then close it again. *Oh God, the press.* They will be in a full-on feeding frenzy. A single drop of blood in the water is enough to have them sniffing around. This . . . this was a bloodbath, a massacre of epic proportions for them to feast on. They will be nothing short of brutal.

I look round the room. At the shattered bodies and faces. There is absolutely no one in here who deserves to have to go out in front of the world's media and defend this shambles. I drop my head, take a deep breath and let it out.

'I'll do it.'

'Mac, you don't have—'

'I'll do it, Jabba. Who else is there?'

He doesn't have an answer. I haul myself to my feet and head out to face the music.

As we hobble towards the door, Jabba leans in and murmurs, 'Just so you know, Mac. Our chief selector has been quietly distancing himself from the Thomas selection. He has spoken to a few of his chums in the Press Box, making sure they know that it was you who pushed for his inclusion.'

'Brilliant,' I mutter.

I limp out of the dressing-room door and head for the stairs. Looking down, I notice just how filthy my whites are. Still soaked in sweat, stained and bloodied and stinking to high heaven. If Reg manages to get these anywhere near clean, I'll revise my opinion of him.

'Hi, Mac. Excuse me, sorry.'

I'm not really in the mood to stop for a selfie or an autograph, but I try to never say no, so I stop and turn on the stairs and look up to the man who has called out. To my surprise I find I'm looking at a familiar face. I have barely seen him in years, not since he was fifteen and I was coaching him in the nets in my gap year.

'Johnny Watson.' I hold out my hand. 'How are you?'

'Didn't think you'd remember me.'

I shake my head. I probably would have anyway, he was always a singular character, but he has also led a fairly glittering career since I knew him, and I have had regular updates from Dad and others. Watson now runs a hedge fund in Switzerland; probably worth more than the ground we are all standing in.

'How long have you been back in the country?'

'Flew in this morning' *On the company jet, no doubt.* 'Got

141

an invitation I couldn't refuse from this old bufftey,' he nods to the man in the blazer and MCC tie walking over to join us.

'Beats!' I grin, stepping forward to greet one of my Dad's oldest friends and my ex-housemaster.

★

Will Beattie, Beats to all who knew him, was one of those schoolmasters they don't seem to make any more. A figure of myth and legend in his small world, respected by his colleagues and adored by successive generations of boys who passed through the school.

Not particularly adept in the classroom, but a veritable horse-whisperer with his adolescent charges outside of it. His boarding house had always been the most oversubscribed and the most successful, and I loved my five years there.

He seemed to have the happy knack of catching the boys behaving well. Even the most dissolute members of his house – the lazy, feckless, prematurely cynical ones – would, on the rare occasions when they were doing something right for once, suddenly notice Beats beaming over their shoulder. 'Well done, McGregor', followed by a small word of praise that felt like trumpets sounding and a crowd cheering inside the small boy's chest, and then a comment, comparing him favourably to the elder brother in whose shadow he'd lived for ever, that would glow inside him for a week.

Faced with a scowling rugby coach, irate that a boy in his house had 'ruined' his chances for Saturday by skipping practice again, Beats would smile apologetically, reassure him that whilst there had clearly been some innocent misunderstanding, he would speak to the boy and it wouldn't happen in future.

The Test

Later the miscreant would be called into his study, and informed that Mr Wilson, a really top-notch coach, was *very pleased* with the way you've played this term, and *thinks you have an excellent chance of making the 1st XV* if you continue to make such progress. Unfortunately, he seemed to be under the – *I am sure mistaken* – impression that you missed practice yesterday. I assured him you were there and that he probably missed you because you were running so fast but, either way, the best thing would be to make sure you are there particularly early for the next couple of weeks and train your absolute hardest so that he doesn't forget that you're there again. And I feel bad for not having seen you play in ages, so I'll make sure I pop out to watch you at some point. I haven't seen you in action since you scored that try in the house final last season.

The boy would depart feeling simultaneously proud, relieved, and as if he had been check-mated in a game of chess he hadn't known he was playing.

Saturday 7.46 p.m.

There are still half a dozen people around when I finally make it back into the dressing room, feeling like a human punchbag. The assembled representatives of the fourth estate have just vented the collective frustrations of an entire nation on me. And in the morning they will undoubtedly drag my reputation into a gutter and kick the shit out of it.

'The most shambolic day's play in recent memory'; 'A shameful performance'; 'Inept and indefensible. England were a disgrace!'

The dressing room looks like a bomb's hit it. Rubbish – dirty cups and plates, along with the cellophane bags in which our kit comes – lies strewn everywhere. 'Where the hell's Reg?' I ask. Not for the first time that day.

On the TV in the corner is a Hawk-Eye graphic showing Casey's plays-and-misses. A slow-motion montage is dissecting his technique in minute detail, from angle after angle. In the voiceover an ex-player is slagging him off. 'Mistake that has cost us the Ashes'; 'Not good enough, shouldn't have been picked, not ready for this level'; 'Fundamental flaws in his method'; 'If you look at Thomas's feet, he gets no sort of stride in'; 'he plays with his hands much too wide of his body . . .'

Grub picks up the remote, 'Where's the footie highlights?' he says casually, and changes the channel, cutting off the character assassination.

I sit down next to Casey. 'Ignore all that bollocks. Your technique's fine. Just play the game that got you selected. You're good enough. That's why you're here. You belong at this level, and don't let anyone tell you otherwise.'

He nods, his eyes never leaving the telly. I put my hand on his shoulder for a moment and then limp away to the shower.

'Dance with the girl you came with.'

My batting coach since I was at school has been an old Gloucestershire player called Jim Stock. This is one of his mantras.

When you first come into the international arena, everyone scrutinises your game, picks out the things you do that are most different to the accepted norm, and tells you it's wrong. If you get out more than once in a certain way, they call it a weakness, and decide some aspect of your technique causes it. *Got to change that. Got to improve in that area.*

As if orthodoxy were any guarantee of success. As if this were the moment for you to start changing your technique.

'When you get to the big show, Mac, you are better to dance with the girl you came with.'

Keep things simple. Trust the game that got you here, back yourself and the instincts and techniques you've spent years honing. Don't overreach, feeling you have to do something special. Adapt to the threats coming at you, but within the bounds of your capabilities, not outside them.

Orthodox technique is a chimera anyway. Bradman's grip. Lara's backlift. Would anyone coach those? If you saw a kid with either of those, what would your first instinct be?

Gap year, back at school

And the pathos never touches them.

'Shot! Nice balance, Watson.' I wipe the sweat from my eyes and pick up the bucket. Watson takes off his helmet, and he and I start to collect the balls.

One of the younger teachers comes stumbling past the nets. Will Cripps, with his nervous little twitches, scrawny physique, and prematurely middle-aged haircut and outfits is a caricature of academic nerdiness. Even his walk, slightly off balance and syncopated, looks as though he learned it from a book; he proceeds with a look of intense concentration, as if he is trying to recall the memorised instructions.

Next to me, Watson is smirking at him openly.

'He's a nice man, Mr Cripps,' I intercede on his behalf. 'A good teacher, too. Incredibly bright.'

Watson specialises in that benign form of terrible behaviour that seems to be an almost inevitable corollary to the good-hearted-yet-bored subset of boarding-school boys, and he has the precocious intelligence to do so without getting caught. He understands the school rules, and the need for them, and the reasons why the school has to have them, but he refuses to accept the basic premise that they apply to him.

'I know sir. I've got him for Chemistry.' He grins. 'We've trained him to stand in the corner, you know.'

'You've done what?'

'Trained him, sir. To stand in the corner.'

'What do you mean?'

'Behaviourism, sir. Whenever he starts talking we ignore him, stare out of the window, don't know anything, don't look interested.' He slouches into the archetypal sulky teenager pose. 'Then, if he moves in the right direction, we start to look interested. Once he's in his corner, we're like this.' He leans forward, miming puppy-eyed enthusiasm. 'We smile at him, laugh at his jokes, and answer his questions.' I'm shaking my head in disbelief, although I don't doubt that every word is true.

'It took us a week or two to break him in, but now he starts the lesson and goes straight to his little corner. We're nearly ready for Phase Two, sir.'

'Phase Two? No.' I hold up my hand. 'Don't. I don't want to know.'

'There's this big cupboard, right above the corner, where—'

'Watson. I don't want to know.'

'Well sir, in my own modest opinion—'

'Modest, Watson?' I cock an eyebrow.

'Yes, sir. Modesty is one of my finest, and most under-stated, qualities,' he continues, without missing a beat.

'Put your helmet on,' I say more firmly. 'We're going to do a bit of work on the *short* ball.'

The Test

This, at least, is some small revenge that I can take on Mr Cripps's behalf.

The first ball ricochets off his helmet. *Get that up you, you rascal.*

Saturday 8.07 p.m.

Back in the dressing room, I slump into my seat.

A text pings into my phone. It is from Rob, our absent captain, still sitting in Leeds in his hospital bed.

Ignore them fuckers. You're doing fine. Keep going. Good luck, Rob

I look across the room to his empty spot on the far wall.

He is genuinely a person apart, our captain; different both in kind and degree to anyone I've known. It is difficult to describe, hard to capture his presence well enough for someone who has never met him to understand. He is the centre of any room. So solid he makes the world around him fainter, like an explosion of power at rest.

It's the eyes that tell you first.

The eyes say, *I see you.*

And the Viking arms, that could sack the monastery at Lindisfarne, then pull an oar for a day and not notice.

His handshake is like two feet calmly planted on firm ground. Whatever it is that comes before Alpha.

The eyes come and meet you just your side of halfway. *I see you*, they say.

The Test

Don't get me wrong. He is no angel.

Off the field, away from the dressing room, he has his flaws. Jabba spends much time and effort keeping his worst excesses out of the papers.

But in here, he is rudder, and compass, and engine.

The whole team, different and disparate, most of them older than he is, follow him without a thought. Without question, without doubt, without fear.

I look at his cap on its peg: sun-bleached, sweat-stained.

There is no faking this. No mimicking him. I simply don't have the option of captaining his way. This is going to have to be my tune.

As I limp out of the dressing room, I bump into an old friend. A guy I overlapped with for a couple of years in the England team. Now he commentates and writes a column in a daily paper. It is nice to see a friendly face, but I soon realise that he is looking sheepish, and as we start to chat he is clearly trying to get his excuses in early.

Weary beyond belief, I sigh and do my best to let him off the hook, 'Look mate, we're having a mare. I know you've got a job to do. Write what you need to write. I don't have a problem with you telling it as you see it.' *I do, of course . . . a bit, but what's the point in losing a good mate? It's not going to help anything now.*

Grub drives me back to the hotel.

We pull out of the ground and turn left. At the end of the road we are stopped at the junction by a red light, right next to a group of yellow-shirted Australian fans. One of them spots us, and points us out to his mates, who roar delightedly and start chanting in our direction.

Another, who has clearly had more to drink than the others, runs over to the car and stands in the road right next to the driver's door. He bounces up and down, screaming abuse and gesturing obscenely with both hands.

When he gets no reaction, he presses himself up against the glass of the side window, and continues to bellow at us.

Grub stares straight ahead, impassive. The Aussie is a bare twelve inches from the side of his head, his face and two-fingered salute pressed up against the glass. He leers his drunken, triumphant grin, and keeps up his stream of foul-mouthed abuse. For what feels like an age we sit there, waiting for the lights to change. The oaf keeps bellowing. Grub's expression doesn't move a millimetre.

Eventually he just mutters, 'Brilliant!' under his breath. 'Now our day's perfect.'

DAY FOUR

Gap year

So here I am, every afternoon and all day Saturday, throwing balls in the nets at school.

I pick up the ball, nestle it into the baseball mitt on my left hand, and sight the target at the other end of the nets. Then, when the boy is ready, two steps, and a long, lazy loop of my arm, the ball sails out in a gentle half-volley. The bat goes up, starts to come down straight, starts to describe the arc that it should make through the ball, but then his bottom hand takes control, skewing the blade sideways and closing the face, destroying any margin for error. If he is a little out in his timing, he'll miss the ball. He is and he does. The back net billows as the ball hits it. The boy grunts in frustration.

I'm desperately trying to hit the middle of the bat.

In the neighbouring net, Stocksy is throwing at another of the boys. I love working with him. He has been at the school for twenty years, and has coached me since I was nine years old. Even as a pro, I'll go back to him as my first port of call when I feel my game isn't right.

We throw for hours, side by side. My arm tires, then gets sore, then feels as if it will fall off. Stocksy, next to me, never flags. Calmly keeping up a gentle but consistent pressure on the boys to get a little bit better than they were. Always pushing them forward, nudging them out of their comfort zone.

Your comfort zone's a nice place to be, but nothing grows there, Mac.

Humble, gentle, generous to a fault. If he had an ego I never saw any trace of it. But at the same time he was hard. Looking at him as a kid it felt as if he must have been forged, not born; iron, and not just on the surface: iron all the way through. I never saw him take a backward step, or an easy option. Never saw him cut himself one inch of slack. Never heard him mention his nearly thousand wickets for Gloucestershire, not even once. He did it right, the way he thought it should be done, every time. He played the longest of long games, and rarely lost.

He and my Dad ran the cricket together for years. They were a great pair. Dad the poet, the jazz-lover, with his Celtic passions never far below the surface: all fire and air. He wore his heart on his sleeve; lived and breathed the matches. Celebrated the wins, held his head in his hands at the defeats.

Stocksy, the West Country farmer. Grounded in the deep Gloucestershire soil, and the long rhythms and deep cycles of agricultural life: earth and water.

Enthusiasm, literally the inhalation and absorption of the divine. Both men were filled by it, in their different ways. Dad, all bright-eyed energy, able to make a fielding practice in the rain the most fun the boys had all week. Stocksy, calm, solid as bedrock, with the patience to outwait Time itself.

Stocksy throws.

In the next net along, I prattle. 'Shot! . . . Bad luck, maybe a bit too much bottom hand . . . Yes, watch your balance, just falling over a little . . . Keep coming at the ball . . . Come on, really watch it onto the bat.'

Next door, Stocksy just keeps throwing.

Then he wanders down the net, takes the bat from the boy's hands. Shows him what he wants him to do, shows him what he's doing at the moment, then shows him again what he wants him to do. Then he goes back to throwing.

I keep prattling. 'Make sure you're clearing your hands . . . Left elbow high.'

Yet, somehow, the boy I'm working with hasn't managed to incorporate the nine technical changes I've asked him to make in the last five minutes.

Maybe he's just not trying.

After the boys have left, mine apparently worse than when he arrived, I go over to Stocksy.

'What am I doing wrong?'

'You're doing all right, I reckon.'

'But he got worse. I couldn't get his bat coming down straight for love nor money.'

'Too much bottom hand?'

'Yeh. It was the only thing we worked on.'

'So you started with what he couldn't do?'

'Is that wrong?'

'There's no right or wrong. But maybe let him feel a few out of the middle first next time. We all tighten up when it's not going well.'

'OK, I'll start with some easy ones next time.'

'Look, some days they get better, some days they don't. Keep throwing balls and they'll improve eventually.'

'You're saying progress isn't linear.'

'I don' reckon I know what that means.'

Progress has not followed a straight ascending line, but a spiral with rhythms of progress and retrogression, of evolution and dissolution. Stocksy would have got on well with Goethe.

★

At the end of each evening's coaching, Stocksy would tidy away the kit and then go to the fridge at the back of the pavilion and get us both a beer. We'd sit and watch the sun dropping towards the river.

We are sitting there one evening when he clears his throat. 'Have I told you the story of the player in the hole?'

When I shake my head, he begins: 'A player was practising one day when he suddenly fell into a big hole. He tried to get out, but no matter how hard he tried, he couldn't get enough grip, and eventually he had to admit that he was stuck.

'After a while, one of his coaches wandered by. "You've fallen down a hole," he said. The lad thought that was fairly obvious, but the coach went on. "Now what you wanted to do there was to see the hole before you got to it: that way you'd be able to adjust and think, *There's a hole, I'll walk somewhere where there isn't one*," and with that advice he left, leaving the player stuck.

'After an hour or two, another coach walked past.

'This coach looked at the player in the hole and said, "Oh no! You've fallen in a hole. Well, you won't be able to play on Saturday if you're stuck in that hole, will you?" and so he wandered off to pick a player who hadn't fallen in a hole to play instead.

'The player sat in his hole, getting colder and colder, and more and more fed up, until eventually a third coach

158

appeared. This coach looked at the player in the hole and started to get annoyed. He shouted at him, telling him that he needed to try harder, that he just didn't want it enough, and that if he was really serious about succeeding, he wouldn't be falling in holes. To be honest, by doing so, he was letting himself and his team down and he, personally, was very disappointed by this "falling into holes" behaviour. Then he wandered off to the bar and told increasingly long stories about other players he knew who'd fallen in holes and pointed out several times that when he'd played, he'd never fallen in a hole.

'The player sat shivering in his hole as night fell, when at last a fourth coach happened to walk past. This coach took one look at the player and jumped down into the hole next to him.

'"Oh, but that's the stupidest bloody thing that any of you have done," said the player in exasperation. "Now we're both stuck in here."

'"Yes," admitted the coach, "but I've been in here before, and I know the way out."'

It is, by a factor of ten, the longest thing I have ever heard Stocksy say. We sit for a while in silence, sipping our beers.

'So you've gotta get in the hole with them,' I say eventually.

'You do,' he nods, 'else why would they ever trust you?'

Cricket was always poetry to Dad, and therefore to me. He loved his football and his rugby, like any good Scot. They were exciting and action-packed. They had their own beauty and style, but they were prose. Cricket, though, cricket was poetry.

There is a spot, above the 1st XI pitch at school, where he would take his notebook, instal himself on his favourite bench and, staring down at the crisp turf, sit and write for hours.

I am standing at his shoulder as he writes, black ink, on clean white sheets. By his side is his morning's work, a neat pile of pages, each covered in his looping script.

I flick through them.

'You've written a lot.'

He smiles, then frowns in concentration as he goes back to the writing, trying to get some elusive thought down before it slips away.

'How do you write so much?'

He finishes, puts his pen down. 'One word at a time,' he says drily and, when I snort, he continues, mock serious, 'No, honestly, I've tried doing two at a time and all the letters get muddled.'

I laugh. 'I find it hard. Don't know how to start.'

I still think this is what I'll be when I grow up, a writer.

'The tyranny of the blank page,' he smiles. 'Just write something. Then work out what it's supposed to be later.'

'Can we play cricket?'

'Tell you what. You help your mum hang up the washing, I'll finish this, and then we'll go to the nets.'

Colombo, six years ago

'There's always an arsehole.'

'There doesn't have to be.'

'No, there doesn't *have* to be,' Grub admits, 'but there always is one. Someone will always be the arsehole, no matter how many you drop, or who you pick. Some are worse than others, and you can have more than one, but there's always one in every team. It's just how it works.'

A wicket falls, and we unglue ourselves from our plastic chairs on the boundary edge and jog out to the middle. The player we've been discussing is our Not Out batsman. He takes the towel from me, wipes his face and neck, and swaps his gloves for the dry pair I've brought out. Then he takes the water bottle that Grub offers him and takes a swig.

'Fuck's sake!' he shouts, spitting the water straight back out again in disgust. 'Too cold!' He thrusts the bottle back into Grub's hands and struts away, muttering. We turn and jog off, wishing the incoming batsman luck as we pass him. As soon as we are out of earshot, Grub mutters: 'See . . . arsehole!'

The Test

'Oh, I'm not arguing about him. I'm just saying that if you left him out, the rest are basically all right, no tossers.'

We get back to our chairs. I drop into mine. Grub peers carefully around his for a few moments, checking under bags and nearby benches, then lowers himself into it.

'I'm fucking melting here.' He takes a swig of water. 'How can it be too cold?' he asks exasperatedly.

We are both running with sweat in the Colombo heat. The humidity has been brutal all trip, and from the moment you step outside in the morning, you are slick with sweat. 'That bloke's wearing a sweater!' he says, pointing at one of the handful of locals sitting in the stand behind us. 'Why does anyone in this country even *own* a sweater?' Grub shakes his head and returns to his earlier subject.

'Every team has at least one of each. There's always an arse-hole. There's always a fool. There's always a know-it-all . . .'

And Grub proceeds to lay out his theory, whilst keeping a furtive eye on the ground around him. One of the players will have been around for longer than the others, or have had more success, and he'll let his ego run. Throw his weight around; bully the others because he can. He's difficult to rein in, and those in charge find it easier to make the odd allowance. The more his behaviour is overlooked, the more it is tacitly accepted, and the more he pushes the line. Now he's acting like a proper arsehole. Sooner or later, he becomes more trouble than he's worth, because he gets out of hand, or his form deteriorates, or the management changes. Either way, eventually he gets left out.

Then there's a void.

You can have one. You can make allowances for one, and it doesn't affect things too badly.

163

So now the next biggest dog looks around, and finds there's a bit more room for his ego. He flexes his muscles a little, finds he gets away with it. *Hey presto! New arsehole.*

I nod at our compatriot in the middle. 'Can't believe he ever *wasn't* the arsehole. He's the original spherical bastard.'

'Amen to that.'

I glance down at Grub's trouser bottoms, which are tucked into his socks despite the heat.

'I don't think that's going to help, you know.'

We had a large snake slide straight under our chairs yesterday. The locals reckon it was a cobra. They seemed surprised that we don't have cobras at our cricket grounds. Very useful, keep the rats down.

'Aw man! They give us the willies,' he says, eyes flicking to the hole in the ground down which the snake had disappeared the day before.

'You know the anti-venoms don't work very well over here?'

'Say what?'

'They're based on the Indian varieties; they don't work very well on the Sri Lankan subspecies.'

'You just made that up! Right, Mac? Mac . . . you just made that up, right?'

'The pitch has done a bit more this morning, don't you think?' I say, gazing out into the middle.

'Mac!?'

*

'Jeez, he's a miserable prick, isn't he? Do you reckon it's because they never made him captain?'

'No, that's bollocks. He's playing cricket for England, for fuck's sake. He's got nothin' to moan about.'

The Test

Grub is carefully placing the wet gloves on the ground, palms up so they will dry in the sun, then he hangs the damp towels over the back of the spare chairs. I am refilling the drinks and putting them and the ice towels back into the ice-box.

'Anyways, people are just happy or sad. S'got sod-all to do with who they are or what they've got, it's just in 'em. No miserable bugger ever won the pools and was transformed into a happy bloke, was he? People have good things or bad things happen to them, they get happier or sadder for a bit, and a year later they're back to where they always were.

'We've all met them, haven't we? The guys who've got everything you could wish for, but who never get round to telling their face. They live lives most people dream of, but walk round looking like someone just ran over their dog.

'They're always just waiting for one last thing, and then they'll be happy. For the promotion, for the bigger car, for the kids to leave for university, for retirement. That's all they want, just that one more thing.

'It's bollocks. It never happens.'

*

We step out into the subcontinental fug. Tuk-tuks honk past at speed; the humidity rolls over us like jet-wash. The noise and the off-sweet, decaying air of a tropical city, acrid with diesel fumes, is overpowering.

'We're not in Kansas any more, Dorothy,' I mutter to myself, revelling in the hot chaos of colour and strangeness around me.

'When were we in Kansas?'

'Shut up, Tayls,' someone says.

Gap year, back at school

My U15 team are playing their annual grudge match against their biggest rivals. They have been talking about it all season. They lost a close one last year, and they and I are equally desperate to do better this year.

I am standing around on the boundary twenty minutes before the start. My opposite number is vigorously engaged in warming his team up: running them round, leading the stretches, hitting catches and giving the pre-match team talk. I normally leave all that to the boys, but I feel like – just this once – I should get more involved. Make sure they are in the right frame of mind for the big match.

I have just barely started to take a step forward, when I hear a familiar voice say, 'Don't you dare, McCall.' Will Beattie is at my shoulder. Reading my mind, as always.

'Now, *you* have your say all week. They have to shut up and listen and do what you tell them. But Saturday . . . Saturday is *their* day.

'On Saturday you have to shut up, and let them play. Saturday is when you find out if all those things you said during the week were worth saying. If they weren't, then there's nothing you can do to put it right now anyway.

The Test

'You have to let them play. You have to let them do it on their own. Where's the point in the whole exercise if you don't? How do they ever learn?' He glances sideways at me. 'Are you nervous?'

'A bit.'

'Well you bloody look it. Try to relax. If you can't, then at least pretend. And if you can't pretend to relax, then go and hide somewhere. Don't pass your nerves on to them.'

I take a deep breath, force a smile, and let the tension slide out of my face.

'On another note,' he says with a twinkle in his eye, 'I heard the most extraordinary story about Mr Cripps's lesson this morning.' *Ah, I might know something about this.*

'Apparently, he was teaching half of this lot,' he nods at my team, 'when a masked boy burst through the door and attacked him ...' I keep my face impassive. '... only for a different boy dressed as Spiderman to drop out of the cupboard above him and drive the attacker out of the classroom.'

He looks me in the eye. 'You wouldn't know anything about that, would you?'

I glance over to where Johnny Watson is throwing into the keeper's gloves.

'No ... nothing ... What a bizarre thing to happen.'

'Well, just remember, *Caesar's wife must be beyond reproach.*' He turns to leave. 'Best of luck for the match, Mac.'

Sunday, 7.10 a.m.

I had set my alarm for a late rise, but the sound of texts pinging into my phone wakes me anyway.

I know what they are before I look.

Hang in there, mate. Don't let the bastards grind you down, Mark

Are you OK? Call if you need to chat. Let me know if there's anything I can do. Sis

Chin up kid. It'll pass – Stocksy

We love you James, Granny

Sounds like people have read the papers.

I try to sit up and my whole body screams at me. I am aching and sore in almost every part I can identify. For a minute or two I'm genuinely not sure I'm going to make it out of bed. Eventually I lever myself upright, and my knee promptly folds under me. I collapse back on to the edge of the mattress again.

Come on Mac, get a grip.

★

I pull into the car park at Lord's and phone home. Sam is more monosyllabic than normal.

The Test

'How was school?'

'Fine.'

'What did you do?'

'Dunno.'

'Are you OK?'

'Fine.'

I can hear Beth in the background but she doesn't come to the phone.

It is left to Emily of all people to explain. 'Daddy, Sam had a fight at school. Th'other boys said mean things about you and Sam did hit them. Then he had go and see Mrs Dean.'

I open my mouth, but I can't talk.

'Daddy? Mummy did cry lots.'

There is a lump in my throat that I can barely talk around. 'Emily, can you put Sam back on please? Emily?'

'I think we got go with Granny n' Bapa now, Dada. Bye bye.'

'Love you, Emily,' but the line is dead.

I close my eyes and rest my head against the steering wheel, my breath coming short and fast.

The text messages are beeping into my phone at a fair rate still. I check them as I leave the car and find the two clinchers:

Tough times don't last, tough people do.

And two different versions of

Form is temporary, class is permanent.

Wow, it must be bad. They must really be whaling on me.

I don't read the press, particularly during matches (for much the same reason that I don't put a bag over my head and then punch myself repeatedly in the face). *I* don't read the press, but unfortunately everyone else I know does. Inferring what's been written about you by the messages of support you get is almost worse than reading it yourself.

I check in with Jabba as I reach the rooms. He gives me a quick summary without anything too specific. Most are waiting for the match to finish before they deliver the *coup de grâce*. But a couple of the tabloids have taken the gloves off already. 'Disgraceful', 'Laughing stock', 'Travesty', 'Pitiful farce', that sort of thing.

Ho hum. I knew it wasn't going to be good.

By the way they are talking about the change in the batting order, it looks like Tayls has got a version of the story friendly to him out there. He just can't help himself sometimes; he'll have just dropped the odd pointed comment into the waiting ear of a friendly journalist. I can't summon the energy to get too irritated by it. In any event, it's now going to be a race to see who strangles him first, Jabba or Grub.

Hero or Villain, Hero or Villain. There aren't many days in between. I've never really understood why my successes or failures with the bat are imbued with such moral weight. Why the strength or weakness of my forward defence on any given day is used as evidence of my character, or lack thereof.

One day –

Run up, bowl, ball pitches, I play the line, the ball seams, snick, catch. Shower time. Fool, idiot, coward. Villain.

Next day –

Run up, bowl, ball pitches, I play the line, the ball seams, missed it. Keep batting. Genius, stout heart. Hero.

Next day –

Run up, bowl, ball pitches, I play the line, the ball seams, etc., etc.

'The uncanny valley' is a phrase from robotics and virtual reality. It refers to a feature of our brains when we encounter the near-human.

As simulations become more real, as humanoid robots become more lifelike, we like them more and more. The closer the simulation is to human, the happier we are with it, the warmer our feelings towards it.

Up to a point.

But then there is a sudden downward turn in the graph. This is the uncanny valley. As things become nearly human, they abruptly start to engender unpleasant feelings in us, they become spooky. We find them unpleasant. This is the uncanny-ness of the uncanny valley.

We are spooked by anything that is nearly real, but demonstrably not.

So we are not good with flawed heroes. We have to believe our heroes are either perfect, or unworthy. The flaw destroys the whole. The overall effect is worse than if they had had nothing going for them in the first place.

My darling James

It is hard this. So hard. To say goodbye when I am not ready.

If you are reading this, then I am gone. And the thought that I am no longer there for you breaks my heart.

Know that I loved you, more than life itself, from the moment I first held you in my arms, until my last breath. And although I am gone, I will always be in your heart, as you were always in mine.

Look after your dad for me. This will be hard for him, harder than I can bear.

And trust your heart. You have a good heart, James – and it is not just a mother's conceit to say that. I never saw you consciously do a cruel or unkind thing, even when you were small. You have always done the right thing, even when it was not easy. You have always made me so proud.

To me, you will always be that boy, with the light in his eyes, running and grinning, sun in your hair, bat in your hand, across the field. Don't lose that boy James. Don't lose that light. Remember why you do it, and when you are ready, step away. The world outside the boundary is full of wonders too.

Goodbye my James. I know you will be OK. Know that you are loved. Trust your heart. And keep running in the sunshine.

Mum

The Test

I fold the well-worn sheet of paper and, feeling the touch of a vanished hand, tuck it back into the pocket at the back of my cricket bag.

Across the room, Grub bangs his way through the dressing-room door looking filthy with anger.

'. . . got cut up by some prick in an Audi. It was a . . . what do you call it? . . . like an R8 but with the flatter back . . .'

'TT?'

Grub transforms before our eyes, the fake anger gone, a grin erupting across his face.

'Oh, go on then, lad, if you're making one. Milk and one for me, please.'

Jabba comes over, plants a cup of tea in my hand. 'You look a bit less dusty than yesterday. No more aberrations?'

I smile grimly. 'No. Back on the wagon.'

'I feel sorry for you teetotallers. You wake up in the morning, and that's the best you're going to feel all day.'

'Churchill, Jabba?'

'Probably,' he shrugs.

'Well, better than misquoting Wittgenstein at me like you usually do.'

He grins, and intones solemnly, 'The world is everything that is the case.'

I glance up in the direction of the scoreboard. 'Then I think I prefer Churchill.'

'OK. If you're going through hell . . .' He nods, leaves the line for me to finish.

'. . . Keep going. I know.'

I look at him. He looks terrible, even for him.

'You OK, Jab? You don't look too clever.'

'Ah, don't worry about me; nothing a heart attack and an early death won't fix,' he snorts.

Just then his phone rings. We have to hand ours in, he doesn't. He picks up, listens, then hands it wordlessly to me. I take it into the back office, closing the door behind me.

'Mac?'

'Beth?'

'Are you OK, sweetheart?'

I love talking to her on the phone. I love the sound of her voice. The way it hasn't changed since we met. I close my eyes, phone pressed to my ear, and we are back together in the darkness, high in the Cambridge rooftops. Folded into each other, skin on skin, breathing each other's breath. Murmuring back and forth in our own private universe, grinning together into the gloom.

'Yes . . . I'm OK. I'm fine.'

'Mac!'

'No, really. It's bad . . . I'm hating it. But it'll pass. I'm OK . . . don't worry.'

'We were watching. They were . . . horrible . . . they . . .' She tails off. Probably realising that I don't need a blow-by-blow on how they are slagging me off.

'I'm just . . . I'm just sorry, Mac . . . It's not fair. You don't deserve it.'

'It is what it is. There's nothing I can do except ride it out.'

'Still . . .'

'In a month it'll be some other poor sod somewhere else, and I'll be on a beach. In a year no one will remember.'

With a sinking feeling I have a sudden thought. 'Beth, have you been getting calls?'

'A few . . .' There's a pause. 'Nothing too bad.'

This comes straight through my defences. I go from calm to angry in a breath. The trouble I cause for those I love is always the hardest thing to cope with.

'Cheap bastards.'

'Don't worry, it's OK. Just take care, Mac. Look after yourself, I worry about you.'

'I'm OK. It is what it is.'

The line goes dead. I close my eyes.

In my mind I see her eye rise over the skin of her shoulder. Then she slides away from me, gliding out of the room, movements lazy as silk in the wind.

And she's gone.

I go back to the dressing room, hand the phone to Jabba. He takes it without comment, but then as I turn away he murmurs,

'*Though much is taken, much abides . . .*'

Though much is taken, much abides . . .

Dad and I walk the boundary on a Saturday afternoon. I sweat in the midday heat to keep up with him, arm stretched up to hold on to his hand.

and though
We are not now that strength which in old days
Moved earth and heaven, that which we are, we are;

The grass burns green around us. Match after match stretches away into the blue-bright distance, the players flickering, white flames in the haze.

As we walk, Dad murmurs lines of poetry to me, reciting whichever verse seems most apt to the situation, absent-mindedly, half to himself, his focus consumed by the battle on the field.

I repeat each line, understanding little, but enjoying the feel of the words in my mouth and ears. I match his cadences, echoing his rhythms back to him.

One equal temper of heroic hearts,
Made weak by time and fate, but strong in will

Year after year we will walk together, boundaries in the summer, touchlines in the winter. He can't stand still when his boys are playing.

The Test

Phrases, lines, whole passages sink their roots deep into my subconscious. God knows how many are buried in there, thousands just waiting . . .

. . . to bubble to the surface, years later, like double-edged swords; watching me, passing their cryptic comments and obscure judgements.

The hammer of the sun's heat beats the turf, which burns through my thin-soled sandals.

The air is thick and heavy. The colours can't be bothered, and laze around. Green fading into blue.

To strive, to seek, to find, and not to yield.

Sunday 10.59 a.m.

Australia	348 and 405 for 7 dec
England	179 and 17 for 2 (8 overs)

They meet me halfway to the crease.

'Morning, shithead.'

'How's it feel to be playing your last Test, Mac?'

I nod back, face carefully neutral. 'Gents.'

'Dead man walking! Dead man walking, coming through!'

The sledges are half-hearted. They are just going through the motions. Thankfully I seem to have acquired a reputation for being fairly impervious to it all. But at the first drop of blood in the water, they'll be all over me, so I'm careful to give them nothing.

I get to the middle and take guard. I look around.

Well then, this is it. Nowhere to run, McCall. You're going home with your shield, or on it.

This is the place that, eventually, every batsman finds himself.

Whether you've been abandoned by fortune, let down by your friends, or screwed yourself egregiously.

You end up here.

You end up in a place where you can't argue, you can't

negotiate, you can't spin the facts, and there's no cavalry coming over the hill.

You're left with only one thing that can save you.

Sometimes you pick up your bat because you're told to. Sometimes you pick it up out of habit because that's what you've always done. Sometimes because you want to, for the sheer joy of hitting balls. Sometimes you do it to show off, because it's expected of you, or because you're bored.

But, eventually, you find yourself picking up your bat because you've got nothing else left, no other way out. You have to bat for the life you know.

There are times when you are one innings away from the end.

Whether it's fair or not. Whether you deserve it or not. You have only one way left to defend your career, your future, the person that you are and want to be.

It can put your feet in concrete, make you overthink and second-guess everything. Any number of good players have been paralysed by it, neutered by the pressure.

With me it seems to go the other way. Luckily, it feels like the moment when you think you're going to crash. Everything slows down, and a strange calm descends.

It's like you run beneath full capacity your whole life and then, suddenly, when you need it, all the major equipment comes on-line. I was in a traffic accident when I was at university, and I remember those few moments better than whole months of my life either side.

Powerlessness is what I hate. If I am at least in partial control, then focusing on what I have to do consumes every-thing else.

He bowls, my feet move, the ball thuds hard into the

middle of my bat. There was no moment in which I was moving. Not that I'm aware of. I was still. He bowled. I was in position. There was no transition.

I know that this is where I need to stay. Focused, ready, loose. Sitting in the centre of that stillness that lets my body react. Trust it, don't interfere. Let my training do its business.

I'm getting nothing from Casey. He's not blanking me, it's just that he doesn't engage with anything I say or do. Having seen him around the dressing room, I know he is different with the others. He has a high opinion of himself, but he's not prickly with them – quite good value, in fact. It just seems to be an issue with me.

Grub has a theory. 'He's worked it all out. Rob comes back in; Miller'll be the spare keeper and extra batsman. That leaves one seat on the plane for the two of yous. I dinna think he's got an issue with you personally. He's just not expecting any favours off you, coz he wants your place, like.'

I've always been rubbish at following this type of barrack-room politics. Things happen that I don't understand, arguments break out for no reason that I can see, then Grub explains it all to me later. He is a master at sniffing out the low cunning and private agendas that occasionally crop up in dressing rooms.

'It's like the old joke. Two guys are crossing the African plain when they see a lion coming towards them. One of them stops and starts changing into his running shoes.

'"What are you doing?" his mate says. "You can't outrun a lion!"

'"No," he agrees, "but it's not the lion I have to outrun."'

★

The Test

The two of us had more awkwardness at breakfast this morning. I came down early as usual and the only other person there was Casey. He nodded, and went back to his cornflakes.

'Morning CT, how're you doing?'

'Aw'reet thanks,' he muttered.

'Sleep OK?'

His eyes flashed up, and he stared at me like I'd questioned his manhood.

'Fine,' he said, after an uncomfortable pause, then went back to his cornflakes. One brief death-rattle of an exchange, and then breakfast in silence.

And that's what it's been like from the moment we met up before the Test. Dealing with him is exhausting. Just trying to navigate a conversation is like wriggling through brambles trying not to get pricked.

Not with the others, just me.

I met his parents as I was leaving the hotel, but then understood him even less. They don't seem to fit him at all. Dad's an accountant, Mum a primary-school teacher, both gun-barrel straight, non-sporty; not at all what I was expecting. They couldn't have been more different from their only son if they'd tried.

The fielders are getting into Casey at every opportunity. Standing well within earshot, they chat about him with cocky disdain.

'Why have they sent this clubby? They must have better players than him!'

'Looks the part, doesn't he? Just can't fuckin' play.'

'Looks the part? Looks shit scared.'

'He's shaking like a shitting dog!'

'Don't worry, mate,' one calls over to him, mockingly. 'It'll all be over soon. Then you can go back to your club team.'

I meet Casey in the middle of the wicket. 'Charming bunch of pricks, aren't they?'

He grunts back with a grateful smirk; we punch gloves and go back to our ends.

McKenzie at short leg switches his fire to me.

'Where's your fat mate, Big Mac? The one who smells like low tide.'

I smile at this. Jabba wouldn't take offence, so I'm not going to.

I nod up at the Press Box.

'He'll be up there, making up lies about you to your journos.' I murmur it out of the side of my mouth, just loud enough for him to hear. 'That is unless you really did used to mug old ladies when you were a kid.'

Easy, Mac, stay in your bubble. Don't get sucked in.

But I've clearly touched a nerve, as I meant to.

'Fuck off! Boring prick!' he snarls at me. 'I'd rather shit in my own hand than have to watch you bat.'

I can't resist smiling and looking him up and down. 'Yes, I think I'd have guessed that about you.'

He takes a step towards me and opens his mouth. But then seems momentarily lost for a retort. Instead he claps his hands and roars his encouragement at the bowler, who is getting ready at the top of his mark.

I go back to checking my guard with the umpire.

It sounds banal enough, doesn't it? But it's an art, and one that many professional cricketers are masters of. The art of finding the chink in the armour, the one thing the batsman doesn't want to hear at that moment. The comment that will distract him just enough, get him focusing on something other than the job at hand. And it's one thing to have this stuff snarled at you by some idiot in a park who you don't know and wouldn't respect anyway. But, walking out to bat in your first Test and getting it from guys with a hundred Test caps, men you've watched and admired for years. That carries a bit more weight behind it.

They don't need to break you. It's not like anyone's about to crack and give up. But for most players, the more relaxed they are, the better they bat. They are trying to distract you, to stop you feeling comfortable, to keep pricking the bubble of concentration that you need in order to perform. All they have to do is to induce one mistake, and then they can move on to their next target.

And it will be a little different for each player. Some just get abuse. If they think you are weak or green, they just batter you. With others it's more subtle. They might keep talking up your weaknesses, or your poor form of late. Or they might just chat to you, perfectly friendly, but incessant, stopping you from settling into the concentration you want.

And the TV cameras are on you already. Your career is already on the line. You're already under enough pressure to make some cracks appear. All they need to do is find the right weak spot and push.

You can succeed in county cricket by nailing a niche set of skills and performing them, year in, year out, in similar circumstances. Same grounds, same opponents, same conditions.

The range of threats that the international arena throws at you is far greater. Can you adapt quickly to new and unusual challenges? Batting in Perth, batting in Chennai; they are so utterly different as to almost be different sports. Can you adjust quickly enough to succeed in each new environment?

And can you do it with a million people watching? Hundreds of millions, in some series?

So for some, the ones who can, the 'step up' is no step at all. It's just the same with slightly better players. For others, it can be a gulf that they will never be able to cross.

Some grow bigger as the pressure grows, are inspired to greater heights when the big occasion arrives. Blood quickens, mind sharpens, and they rise higher, the greater the challenge.

Failure sits in the corner of every dressing room, its gaze unblinking. The best can accept it. Become at ease in its presence without trying to ignore it.

Others are unmanned by it; some quickly, some slowly. Many a promising debut has been followed by a steady deterioration in form and confidence as the pressure and scrutiny wear the bright-eyed debutant down, mentally and emotionally. There follows a tightening, just when they need to relax; introspection and negativity when they need faith and trust. We've all seen the walking wickets making their way to the crease, in our side and theirs, desperately trying to fake it, to walk the walk, even if they can't feel it, so focused on the closing door and the dream behind it that they flounder into every obstacle in between.

This morning he's started the way he left off in his first innings. He's driven at two wide ones and missed both. The slip cordon clearly think they are in the game, and their captain has whistled up extra catchers; he has five in there now. There is an interruption while the bowler replaces a damaged boot, and I take the opportunity to go down and talk to Casey.

'I've played here a lot,' I say, gesturing at the ground in general. 'The slope makes the threats at each end quite different.

'The main danger for you at this end is nicking off.'

The slope takes the ball away from your bat, so you're far more likely to nick it than play outside it. Not only that, but gulley and the wider slips are standing two feet lower than you are, so the ball's far more likely to carry to them if you do get an edge.

'So leave well, make the bowler come to you.'

He's good off his pads and down the ground; he needs to look to score there. Put the cover drive away for now.

'I'm not saying block the shit out of it – if you get a bad ball, smash it – but choose the areas where the odds are in your favour.' Drive when it's under your eyes, but don't go reaching for it.

He grunts and goes back to his crease. I shake my head in exasperation and go back to my end. *Arrogant prat!*

But it seems he has listened, although he doesn't want to show it. He is more watchful, leaving well outside his off-stump, and then, when the bowler overcompensates, he clips him neatly up the slope for two. At the end of the over I try again.

'Well played, that's the way. Look, the pressure's on them. They're expected to take wickets, expected to get this finished and over with. The longer they don't, the more they'll get impatient and try to force it. Let them come to us. Give the fuckers nothing.'

I see off a maiden without incident, and Casey plays the next over beautifully. He leaves the first two then gets a fuller, straighter one. He unfurls (there is no other word for it) that gorgeous straight drive, and the ball skips past me, four from the moment it leaves his bat. He blocks one, leaves the next, and then the bowler gets too straight, Casey leans on it into the leg-side, and we are through for three by the time short leg has tracked it all the way to the boundary.

I walk down the wicket to him. He taps gloves with me, and smiles begrudgingly. 'OK then, coach,' he rhymes it with torch. 'What'z ah do at this end?'

'The slope brings most balls back into you, putting the stumps into play.'

Bowled and LBW are the biggest threat. I tend to trigger further across my stumps, make sure I get a good stride in if I can; that way, if I miss it, I've got a good chance of getting hit outside the line. On the other hand, the wider balls don't offer the same threat this end.

'If they offer you width, then you can go at it. Get that square drive of yours out of the bag whenever you get the chance.'

He nods, 'OK, Mac. You're the expert.'

We bat for an hour without incident. I am solid, watchful but busy. I've found a nice rhythm, my feet are moving well, and I feel like I've got time. Casey is playing beautifully at the other end, all loose-limbed fluidity and easy power. You can see exactly why he has sparked such interest from everyone on the county circuit. Batting like this, he looks the real deal.

After drinks, they change the bowling. Spin from one end, seamers from the other. The hardness has gone from the ball, the pitch is still flat and true, and while never completely comfortable, we both look and feel secure. We make it all the way to lunch with a minimum of incident. And walk off to the delighted applause of the crowd after the first session of the match that we can genuinely claim to have won.

I eat lunch in my seat in the dressing room, happy to be alone with my thoughts for a few minutes.

When the others drift back in from the dining room upstairs, Grub is getting into Tayls again.

'You what?'

'Like they say, "Walk slowly but carry a big stick".'

'Tayls . . . literally no one has ever said that before.'

For some reason, unclear to us, an operatic aria is being played loudly in the gardens behind the pavilion.

'Lunchtime opera now, is it?' Grub says grumpily.

'Nothing wrong with a bit of Puccini,' rumbles Jabba from the corner. Which is when, to the amazement of us all, Tayls pipes up.

'It's Catalani,' he says, matter-of-factly.

We all turn to look at him.

'What?' he says defensively. 'It is. It's *La Wally*. Alfredo Catalani.'

Jabba cocks an ear to the window, listens and then nods in agreement, 'I stand corrected.'

Bloody hell, it's like discovering your dog can play the piano.

'You know opera, Tayls?'

'Had to listen to that shit in every car journey when I was a kid. I'm not likely to get it wrong,' Tayls mutters.

'Tayls, you are a man of hidden shallows,' smirks Grub.

In most areas of life, the gulf between competence and excellence is vast, but deceptively so. The fan, the amateur, the keen enthusiast, even, has no *real* comprehension of that gulf. Of the difference between being good, and operating on the very edge of what is humanly possible.

We grow up in school with the idea that the best are like us but a bit better, that they are essentially engaged in the same activity. And in most places that we then live or work, the best we come across are not that much better than we are. Then, when we watch the very best consistently on television, we become attuned to what they do, inured to the wonder of it.

We are standing on one side of the Grand Canyon, the competence side, looking across to the excellence side. And the other side looks much the same as here. And if you spend enough time watching what's happening over there, then your mind starts to see it as normal, and to overlook the vast, yawning, un-crossable chasm in between.

In no area of life is this more apparent than in sport. The speed of a high-class sprinter, the ability of an Olympic gymnast, they beggar belief.

It is hard to hold the chasm in your head. The distance

between someone who has played a game and got quite good at it, and the world-class professional, who started off far better to begin with, and who has dedicated the majority of his life to mastering the skill, with all the advantages of professional support, hardened and tempered by the furnace of international competition. The difference is between the normal, and someone who is genuinely pushing at the boundaries of what a human being can do.

After a whole twenty minutes of watching the Olympic diving, my dad is an expert. The preternatural skill and bravery required to plummet from 35 feet up whilst twisting and somersaulting at eye-blurring speed and yet still enter the water like an arrow punching its own splash down into the depths, is accepted with the comment.

'8.5! Nonsense, that was worth a 7 at most, probably 6.5.'

Two years ago

Sunday, and we walk across the fields to my parents' place, Emily's hand encased in mine the whole way. Her red wellies trample the wet grass across fields of sheep, clambering over stiles, and ploughing the muddy path down by the river.

A low, dark sky has threatened rain but not delivered, adding to the intrepid feeling of the expedition. We have talked about this for ages, and the walk has been days in the planning; it's the first time that we have tackled the four-mile hike to the next village as a family.

Beth has bundled layers on to the kids until they are nearly spherical, then prodded them out of the back gate. I am carrying a couple of good bottles of wine, and a birthday present for Mum in a bag. Sam grumbles a bit, but is quickly shamed into silence by his little sister's enthusiastic progress.

The walk feels like one of those moments that memories are made of. Emily is giggling, Sam has lost his initial reticence and is racing around us like an excited sheepdog. Beth and I talk friends' news and future plans.

As we near Mum and Dad's place, I have to 'take a phone call'. I dawdle, drop behind, my silent phone pressed to my ear, nodding at the pretend conversation. I wave them on ahead of me, knowing that, as soon as they are out of sight, I can dive into the pub round the corner and make an early start. I need a bit more than Dad usually serves up. I down a couple of pints and then follow the rest of them.

'Sorry, I'm late. Just had to take that call. Happy Birthday, Mum!'

I wrap her up in my arms.

It is a dual-purpose get-together. Mum's birthday, and a leaving do for my sister. My brother-in-law's job is taking them off to Australia. They have packed up their things and are leaving in a few days.

In my memory there is a shadow behind Mum's eyes even then. Was that really there? Or has what followed added it to the remembered image? Did she already suspect the worst? Or was she just feeling what any mother would when her eldest child emigrates to the other side of the world.

'Do you think you've had enough?' Beth is at my elbow as I pour myself another glass of wine.

'Last one, eh?'

An hour later, I'm stuck in a corner of the kitchen. My brother-in-law Zac is bending my ear about cricket. I look down mournfully at my empty wine glass. *No joy there.* I scan the kitchen, but the only bottle is empty. Dad will probably open another for lunch, but we are eating late and that could still be a while away. Zac drones on; I've lost all track of the match situation he is describing. *Ah well, desperate times . . .*

I wait for a distraction, and slip out. The living room is

empty and I head towards the drinks cabinet in the corner
for a quick pre-prandial.

'You guys heading down under for the Ashes this winter,
then?'

Damn, he's followed me.

I like my brother-in-law, he's a good enough bloke, but
he is a keen club cricketer, and an Australian to boot. I seem
to spend a remarkable amount of time hearing about his
most recent innings for the local club Second XI.

'Yes, we fly out in a couple of weeks.'

'Better be ready for a long summer!'

Great, getting sledged by my own family now.

'They're a good side,' I agree. 'Very tough to beat on their
own turf. It'll be a challenge.'

'Gotta remember that over there you guys are public
enemy number one. On a par with murderers and drug
dealers.'

Charming.

'A-huh.' I raise an eyebrow. He seems to realise he's got
carried away and aims at something more conciliatory.

. . . And misses.

'How's your prep going?'

'Well, thanks.' *This is a lie.*

"Cause you've been a bit short of runs, haven't you.
Wasn't sure they'd include you in the squad, especially given
your record over there.'

Glad you weren't picking it, then.

'Thing about Australian conditions is, it's important to
leave well.' *Fuck me, is he really explaining this to me?* 'Perth,
Brisbane, it pisses through there compared to here. It's
important to know what to play.'

I've toured there before, you know. But of course, I just nod.

'And you have to be able to cut and pull. If you can't play off the back foot, then you're stuffed. That's why the Poms always struggle – front-foot players, see?'

I'm trying to keep the irritation off my face, and look interested. *Not that he'd notice.*

He presses on, 'Then there's the heat, not—'

'What are you boys talking about?'

My sister has come to my rescue.

'Oh, hey babe, we were just . . .'

'Zac was just telling me how to bat.'

She punches him in the arm angrily, 'Zac!'

Looks like they may have spoken about this.

He rolls his eyes at me as if I've dropped him in it.

Well, maybe stop acting like a knob then.

She pulls him away, 'Come on you, Mum wants to talk to you about Sydney.'

For a second, I think I'm going to get to that drink, but Beth arrives.

'You OK, Mac?'

'Fine. Just getting some coaching from Zac.'

She rolls her eyes sympathetically

'After he'd equated us with murderers, that is. Maybe I should give *him* some advice about *his* job. What does he actually do again? Brand consultant? How is that a job?'

She raises her eyebrows, and puts her hand on one hip.

'Ooh, big talk from a boy who hits a ball with a stick for a living,' retorts my wife, the ex-human rights lawyer.

Better take that one on the chin.

'Fair point,' I say. *Always the danger of marrying someone way brighter than you are.* She wraps her arms round my waist and gives me a squeeze. 'Why don't I ever quit when I'm ahead?' I say, looking down at her upturned face.

'Because you so rarely are, McCall, you so rarely are.' But she smiles to soften the line. *Still on your side, Mac.*

'Come on. Don't give anything he says a second thought,' she says, dimples twinkling, 'then that'll make two of you.

'Now, let's go and join the party. Your dad's being hilarious.'

A week later

She is standing in the kitchen, hands on hips, ticking away.

There's nothing I can do at this point; whatever I do is wrong.

'Hey honey, you OK?' I get a grunt in response.

The pattern is well established now.

A week after I get home, my free pass expires. I cease to be the best person in the world, start getting in the way, interrupting the rhythm that preceded my return.

Then, ten days before I leave, she gets angry, constantly.

She thinks I'm playing at being dad. Turn up, be fun for a few days, an entertaining novelty. Then disappear again. No need to take responsibility. No contribution to the daily grind of school runs, house chores, bedtime stories.

And she's right.

I can see the cracks emerging; see the strain on the bonds that hold us together. But I don't have time to put things right. Don't have time to fix anything properly. I'm slapping whitewash on to a crumbling façade.

Let me take the kids. You get out of the house, go and do something fun.

I'll put the washing on (*if I can work out how to turn the machine on*). You put your feet up, have a cup of tea.

196

Fine for now, says the look I get back. But where are you going to be in a fortnight when I need you? And for the three months after that?

Beth put her career on hold after the kids were born. It was only going to be for a year or so, and then she'd go back part-time. *But I fucked that up too, didn't I?*

Is this it? Says her half of the silence I can't fully fill. Is this why I studied at Cambridge? Is this what I traded my flourishing career for? For the chance to be a single parent for nine months of the year? For an unpredictable, unreliable husband who sees his kids just long enough to disrupt everything, and then pisses off again?

'Shall I cook supper tonight?' I say.

I don't get a response.

★

She never really warmed to cricket; maybe it would have helped a little if she had liked it more. She didn't mind it, other than that it took up so much of my time, but she didn't love it. She liked the fact that I played, was proud of me, and enjoyed my successes, but no more.

She hadn't grown up with it. Music, drama, dance; they were her obsessions as a teenager. Her family wasn't interested in sports, and so it was just never on her radar until I appeared.

In the early days she was content to hang out at Fenner's, sitting on the grass with friends and sharing a drink in the sunshine. Later she would join my parents at Lord's for county matches at the weekend. She loved their company and would suffer the cricket for the pleasure of it. Then when I got picked for England, those first few series were a new and exciting world that was fun to explore.

197

But she never got it, never saw the attraction. She watched far more than her fair share, and she got to know the ins and outs of the game better than some. But it was out of loyalty and support for me. If I wasn't at the crease, then the action held no interest for her. She barely cared who won, except on my behalf.

Then the kids came along and the reordering of our lives left even less time to be interested in watching me play.

I remember three or four weeks after Sam was born, we went out for supper. Sam, tiny in his Moses basket, slept through the whole evening under the restaurant table. *Look*, we said, naïve to the bone, *we might be parents but it's not going to change us.* It did, of course; almost without noticing, you adapt, inch by unseen inch.

Then Emily arrived and we adjusted further and faster. And to our surprise it suddenly didn't make any sense to either of us for Beth to go back to work.

She tried three days a week, for a while, but she never felt like she wanted to be there. She missed the kids. And when I went away on tour, the logistics of juggling her work schedule and nursery pick-ups became a nightmare.

So she put it on hold.

And that was the routine we settled into. Beth at home, me on the road, with periodic bursts of family life.

We plugged away.

Kept getting through the next day, the next week, the next series.

But at no point did it ever feel like it was working.

Sydney, Australia

Sometimes, touring is good.

We spent the afternoon being hosted on a yacht in the harbour. And now we are sitting around the pool, drinks in hand, watching the sun go down over Sydney Opera House.

The warm-up games have gone well. We won. I got runs. Life is good. This is one of *those* moments. One of those 'you know what, I don't think it gets much better than this' moments.

I slip out of the general conversation to pick up the phone and speak to the one person in the world I want to share this with the most.

On the other side of the world, she answers.

She is sitting in a frozen car, waiting for the windscreen to defrost so she can get the kids to school. Sam is kicking off in the background. I start to tell her about my day, but abort within a few words.

'Are you OK?' I ask instead.

'No, actually. The boiler's packed up. They can't get a replacement to us till next week. The house is freezing, and we've no hot water.'

'You're kidding. Aw love, I—'

'Sorry Mac, I need to go. We're late.' The line goes dead.

I look around sadly, at the pool, the sunset, the Harbour Bridge. Powerless and guilty. And now there is another distance between us. The joys I can't share (after all, I'm not entirely stupid).

So, I turn instead to my other life partner.

The others are drinking, why shouldn't I?

I flag a waiter. 'Could I get a VB, please?'

'Sure, mate.'

Twenty minutes later, I remember, very clearly, thinking, *this is all I want* – this gentle euphoria, three-quarters of the way down my first beer, when the world has gently softened.

This is it. This is enough. Just keep everything exactly like this.

But then it's *not* enough. Not for me. *It's never enough.* This much is good; more must be better.

I remember that thought, because it's *all* I remember. The rest of the night is blackness.

Sunday 2.27pm

Australia   348 and 405 for 7 dec
England   179 and 117 for 2 (48 overs)

We continue after lunch in much the same way. The Aussies are finding it difficult to extract any great venom from the docile pitch, and Casey in particular looks extremely comfortable. I still feel good: calm, relaxed, settled in my rhythms.

They've bowled well, but they are trying to pull me wider and I'm refusing to be tempted, so we've hit a temporary stalemate. I haven't scored a run for twenty minutes now. *Fine by me. The less I have to play at, the less that can go wrong.* But it doesn't make for thrilling cricket, and so the fielders and the Aussies in the crowd are getting stuck into me.

The slips in particular are doing their best to goad me into a false shot.

'Come on, Mac, I've got a section of wet paint I want to go and watch dry.'

'Does this count as batting?'

'It's more like a cross between a wake and a hunger strike.'

'Nah! This is what English cricket looks like, like a dog that knows it's going to die'

Chirp away boys! I'm still here.

★

201

Then, between balls, I happen to glance up at the big screen . . . and there he is.

There is a close-up of him reacting to the last shot I played, leaning intently into the balcony rail, one tensed figure in a crowd of relaxed spectators. I know exactly where he is; up in the box of an old friend of his in the Mound Stand. The cameras have done well to find him; he's away from the box with all the other players' families and girlfriends.

Now I need a moment. The bowler is setting off from his mark and my mind is nowhere. I pull away, pointing up at the area above the sightscreen, behind the bowler's arm, waving to an imaginary spectator to sit down and stop moving. I rest the bat against my leg, straighten my helmet strap, refasten each glove, slowly and calmly. I take a full, deep breath. Keep it simple. Watch the ball. Get through the over. Three more balls. *Come on Mac.*

The next ball is wide of off-stump and I can leave it.

Another breath. *Slow, calm. Watch the ball. Get through the over.*

The bowler pauses, and waves square leg back on to the fence. Two men out on the leg-side make the short ball more of a possibility. Or it could be bluff, a way to fix my feet so that the fuller ball has more of a chance of getting through. They've tried that a couple of times already.

Come on Mac, relax . . . breathe . . . watch the ball. If it's short, get under it.

He runs in, bowls. I see it as short, and try to drop under it. But it's fuller than I thought, and I duck straight into it. It hits the side of my head like a hammer, and for a second I don't know where I am. I lose balance and end up on one knee, the hand I've thrown back to stop myself going down has landed a bare inch from the stumps. I stare at it in horror, head ringing, a metallic taste in my mouth.

Fuck you Mac! Fuck you! Jeez that hurts. Players are gathered round me. Something is dribbling down the side of my face. I don't know if it's blood or sweat.

I stand up slowly, tentatively.

Not too bad. I'd feared worse. My jaw hurts, but my head's clearing.

I look up to see our physio arriving on the scene, bag in hand. Both sides' twelfth men are taking the opportunity to run drinks on to the field, and the big screens are replaying the ball in slow motion from every angle they can find. It looks pretty ugly, I have to admit: the ball has thudded into the bottom of the visor and the corner of my jaw. Watching it up there, I'm surprised it hasn't done more damage. But I'm sore, nothing worse.

Wish you'd warned me you were coming, Dad.

'Daddy?'

'Yes, Sam.'

'Why do you wear a helmet, Daddy?' Furrowed brow, earnest little frown.

'Because mean men are paid to hit me on the head, Sam.'

'Why do they want to hit you on the head?'

'Well they don't really want . . . well actually some of them probably do really want to hit me . . . but they're trying to get me out, and they think if I'm worried about getting hit in the head then they'll be able to get me out more easily. So I wear a helmet.'

'That's clever.' Big grin.

'Thank you.'

'Daddy . . . I'm glad you've got a helmet.'

'Thanks, Sam.'

My sister moved to Australia. Then Beth left, moved back to her parents' place with the kids.

A month later, Mum found a lump. Each successive visit, first to the GP then to the hospital, brought worse news. The end came cruelly and breathtakingly fast, with horrible suffering. And it broke something in Dad.

He had three women in his life that he loved, and who adored him. In four months, he lost them all. And somehow it soured the cricket for him. My cricket had nothing to do with Mum or Sis, but it had driven away Beth, and in his heart the three were all entangled; the pain of all their losses somehow got tied to my cricket. He hasn't watched me face a ball since.

Until now.

And there he is, back in his old spot. I don't know why. I don't know what's changed. Has he turned out to see what is likely to be my last-ever Test innings? Did the final chance to see his boy bat on this stage prove too compelling?

OK. I can't really drag this out any longer without leaving the field.

The physio has patched up my jaw, the fielders are back

in their positions. Gingerly, I slide the new helmet on and retake my guard.

Come on, Mac. Head back in the game. Get back into that groove, just you and the ball.

See ball, hit ball. See ball, hit ball.

The last ball of the over sails well over my head and I get a chance to settle my thoughts at the non-striker's end.

My opposite number has decided that this is the signal for them to come heavy at me. Next time I'm on strike, the two men out are joined by a leg-gully and a short leg, and the short balls start to come thick and fast.

No batsman likes a sustained short-ball attack with this sort of field. You've got nowhere to go, and defending safely is hard. Any attacking shot is fraught with danger.

The best thing to do is leave what you can, and ride out the rest. Stay out of the way of it, and let them punch themselves out. This sort of tactic tires the bowlers much quicker than if they were hitting their normal lengths, and they can only sustain it for a fairly short period of time. If you can duck and sway out of the way, and look untroubled by it, then they will hopefully decide not to waste their energies, and move to a different plan. Easier said than done, of course, and what comes next is an unpleasantly quick, hostile fifteen minutes.

I'm getting through it without much incident, until a short ball, into my body, flicks my arm on its way through to the keeper down the leg-side.

There's a huge appeal, taken up by every Australian in the ground. It feels like an age before the umpire shakes his head, Not Out. But now the bowler and captain are at the centre of a huddle.

The Test

Are they going to refer it?

To be honest, I'm not 100 per cent sure myself. One of the endless wrinkles of cricketing law here: glove is out, arm is not. This has hit either the very top of my glove or the arm just above. Some of the fielders are studying me, trying to spot signs of confidence or guilt. I deadpan back as best I can.

No referral. The fielders jog back to their positions, the screen shows a zoomed-in replay of the impact, fractionally above the glove. Safe for now.

When they start paying you, the game is no longer a game. It can take a while to realise, it can take a while to affect you, and for some blessed souls, it never does – they manage to play their whole careers like they are still messing around in the backyard with their mates. But for most people, at some point – normally when you hit a rough period, and the runs dry up – you realise that you are batting for your mortgage. You are batting for your home, your kid's shoes, the car you want to drive, the girl you want to marry and the future you want to have.

You have moved from chasing a wonderful dream to trying to hang on to the things you don't think you can live without. The guy at the other end of the pitch is no longer a fellow traveller in this quirky circus you've both ended up in, he is the bastard who's trying to take away your career, your house and your self-respect.

Eventually, you start to pray for rain.

It sounds ridiculous, but I used to check the forecast hourly, hoping to see bad weather coming our way.

There's no pressure sitting in the pavilion watching it rain. You can't fail there. You go home with the same average you turned up with.

The Test

I heard a line on the radio that summed it up. 'When I was young, ecstasy meant sex. Later it was Wagner. Now it's a cancelled meeting.' A day's play lost to rain was like Christmas come early. (A day's *play*: bloody stupid word for it, I used to think.) And then that thinking spread into everything. Death by a thousand short cuts. Take the easier route. Avoid risk, avoid putting yourself under pressure. If it's optional, don't do it. If it's not optional, cut every corner you can.

It is Stocksy who gets me back into the team.

*

I am sweating in the heat.

'Two!' shouts Stocksy. I sprint up the net, turn and run back, completing the two. My lungs are burning, my legs are heavy. I've been off the booze for a week, but it is still clogging every cell in my body. I've barely started the session, but I'm already gasping for breath. I feel heavy and ponderous. This is the third net I've had in as many days, and it's fair to say that they haven't gone well.

I settle back into my stance. Stocksy throws, I tuck it off my pads, 'Three!' he calls. My legs are still like jelly.

'Tell you what . . .' I pant, not moving. 'Why don't you . . . just throw me . . . a few drives. I just want to feel the ball in the middle a few times.'

He cocks his head. Says nothing. Turns slowly. Goes back to his mark. He loads up another ball and throws me an off-stump half-volley. I drive it into the side net. Then another. And another.

We finish the bucket of balls. Then start to pick them up, in silence.

He's not happy.

'What?' I say eventually.

'You need to get off the bridge,' he says evenly, not looking up, still picking up balls. I wait for an explanation, but get nothing more.

'What do you mean?'

'You're stuck on the bridge and you need to pick a side and get off it,' he says, as if this explains everything.

I stop picking up balls and turn to face him. 'Explain.'

He finishes collecting the last few, then sets the bucket on the ground between us.

'When a kid starts playing, he generally tries to do what the coach tells him. He lets him push him, take him out of his comfort zone.' He shrugs, 'Some players stay that way. Let the coach drive them throughout their career.

'Others take over responsibility. Start to drive *themselves* forward, motivate and stretch *themselves*. Doesn't mean they don't still listen, accept advice. But *they* own the process. Drive it themselves.

'You, Mac, you're stuck on the bridge in between. You've made up your mind that you're too long in the tooth to let someone else tell you what to do, but you aren't ready to drive yourself. You're stuck between the two, going nowhere.'

'I'm struggling here, Stocksy!' I'm angry now, *Fuck does he know?*

'Well . . .' He turns and heads towards the pavilion, taking the balls with him. 'If you want my help, you know where I am.'

'Stocksy!' I call after him. But my pride hears the edge of a whine in my voice, and anger bubbles up again. I throw my bat at the net and rip off my pads.

The Test

We don't talk for a week.

When I do phone him again, I tell him I'm ready to drive.

And I do.

The first thing he says to me when we start is, 'If you don't bleed, you won't heal!'

I nod. *OK then, bring it on.*

Slowly at first, then with growing relish, I rediscover the joy of pushing beyond what is comfortable; of driving myself into the dark, excruciating areas on the edge of my physical and emotional limits.

I stop looking for comfort and start looking for struggle. I make peace with failure, and accept its silent vigil from the corner of every room.

I stop praying for rain.

And as I do it, I become aware of how clogged and polluted I've become; of the rust – mental, physical and emotional – that I've allowed to degrade my brain and body. The cleansing becomes obsessive; the scouring of the toxic sludge from muscles and mind.

I go to India and make runs for the Lions on the 'A' tour. When I come back I train even harder.

Six months later, I'm in the best shape of my career, and when the new season starts, I'm ready to fight for my place.

Sunday 3.23 p.m.

Australia   348 and 405 for 7 dec
England   179 and 169 for 2 (63 overs)

It is getting pretty ugly now.

They've switched up tactics again. Their two best quick bowlers have come back on, and they are going hard at Casey. They have set their field for a barrage of short balls and are hammering him with everything they've got.

And he's getting battered.

Ball after ball is whistling around his head and shoulders. He has worn two on the arm and lid, and gloved one for a lucky boundary, just wide of the diving wicketkeeper. At least two more have flashed past the edge of his bat.

You can't fake confidence in batting. However much you stick your chest out and try to look relaxed between balls, the instinctive, reflexive movements you make in the split second that the ball is in flight betray you. If you're scared or uncomfortable, it shows. And at this level, the opposition don't miss it.

The fielders are gliding past him like sharks scenting blood, surrounding him wherever possible, chipping away verbally.

'Yes, Dicko! Great bowling, mate. Stay there! Won't be long, eh?'

'Not so pretty now is it? Just another weak prick with a cover drive.'

Every fielder who passes within earshot takes a pop. Needling away at Casey's nerve and confidence.

'Does he look scared to you? He looks scared to me.'

'Scared? He looks fucking terrified.'

'I think Daddy forgot to teach him the *short* ball!'

'Nah, he's just piss weak! Nice technique, no ticker!'

'No wonder the rest of his team can't stand him.'

'Fuckin' soft cock.'

I walk down the wicket to talk to him, ostensibly tapping down marks with my bat. His eyes have gone. He is fuming. Rattled by the short ball and riled by their insults, he is desperate to fight back, ready to do something stupid.

'Take it easy, mate,' I say, as relaxed as I can make it sound, smiling and holding his eyes. 'They're just winding you up.'

'I'm not going to last here like this, just standing and taking it. I'm gonna take it on, smash it into the stands.' He glances in the direction of deep mid-wicket.

'That's what they want, Case.' I nod at the deep fielders waiting on the boundary edge. 'They've got three out; they want you to take them on. You might get a couple away, but the odds aren't in your favour.

'Stay calm, and get under it. Duck what you can, get behind the rest. If you give 'em nothing they'll soon lose interest. Their bowlers are hanging out of their arses already, they can't keep banging it in like this all day.'

I go back to the non-striker's end. If I'm honest, I'm not sure what he's going to do. But again, he seems to listen. He gets through the rest of the over by ducking and swaying out of the way. I take the whole of the next one and manage to nick a single off the last ball to keep the strike.

Slowly, ball by ball, over by over, we get through this phase. Eventually their quicks start to flag and they have to try something different.

I walk down the pitch to Casey and punch gloves. 'Well played. Keep going, ten more minutes till tea.'

I have given up trying to understand my technique. Not in despair; in fact, the opposite.

There are moments when I feel like I have lived my whole life in the nets. Day after interminable day. I can close my eyes and be back there in an instant: baking in my helmet, sweat in my eyes, and the stink of my kit in my mouth. Striving, feeling, exploring. Trying to wrestle something I can't quite get hold of, to feel something which I know is there, close by, but tantalisingly just out of reach.

Progress is quixotic. Days of work can amount to nothing – indeed, often make things worse. Then improvements occur suddenly, unlooked for. Not quite a complete surprise, but almost so.

Any time I think I understand the process, I inevitably get worse, not better, and realise I was wrong.

So, eventually, I came to understand that I'm not supposed to understand. That it is not something I *can* understand. *Not consciously.*

To play the perfect cover drive, it is not necessary to *know* how to play the perfect cover drive.

I travel a lot, and so I read a lot. Eventually, I read about Darwin and then I read about Turing. To my surprise, they prove oddly relevant to net practice. In *On the Origin of Species*, Darwin proposes something counterintuitive, an 'inversion of reasoning', if you like; namely that 'to make a complex and beautiful object, it is not necessary to *know* how to make it'. On the contrary, he argues that the *blind competence* of natural selection can result in a perfectly functioning wing or eye, even in the absence of any sentient understanding of either problem or solution.

Alan Turing's work in computational theory consists of a similar inversion: 'that to be an accurate and efficient computing machine, it is not required that you know what arithmetic is'. Turing showed that the finest human calculators could be replaced by a dumb machine, faithfully following sets of simple, nested instructions.

Not only did Darwin and Turing have two of the great ideas in history, but they had in many ways the *same* idea: namely, that *blind competence* can solve a problem in the absence of a coherent understanding of that problem. Which is what brings us back to net practice.

The way in which we learn a complex skill is another instance of that same inversion of reasoning. Refinement of technique is not stimulated by a greater understanding of either the problem or the solution, but by a long iterative process of trial and error. As the mantra goes: *repetitions without repetition*.

The nets then, for me, cease to be a place to be present and become a place to be absent. Practice becomes simply a way of applying suitable evolutionary pressure to the ecosystem of reflexes to which I am host.

I don't know how I hit the ball. But that's OK. I don't need to.

If the purpose of medicine could once be described as

'distracting the mind while the body heals itself', then training is simply a mechanism for keeping the conscious mind sufficiently focused on something for long enough for the subconscious to learn to bat.

No one can understand or explain a process they are in the middle of. Asking someone how they learned something is like asking a bird how it grew its wings, or a toddler how she learned to walk.

When I was at school, one of my teachers had a Yorkshire terrier, which he would take for walks around the village. Whenever he tied him up outside a shop, the dog would bark and bark until he returned.

I asked him once, 'Why does he do that?'

He answered straight away, 'Because he thinks it *works*. He always barks, and I always come back. If you could ask him what made me come back, he'd say, "I did."'

In net practice, we are the dog.

The conscious mind can't hit a ball. All it can do is recognise success when it sees it. Act, essentially, as a cheerleader to the deep circuits, whose blind competence we are seeing the results of.

The conscious mind is not involved, cannot be. When we bat, our movements are literally faster than thought. Our minds are slow, cumbersome things, compared to the reflexes necessary to catch or hit a cricket ball, or even for that matter to keep us upright when we run.

So your subconscious races on ahead and finishes the task, while your thoughts, chugging along behind like some unreliable narrator, merely write themselves into the drama after the fact, giving themselves a prominent role to boot, and taking entirely undue credit for any success.

And here it is worth adding that I do *know* what a cover drive looks like.

I know what a good one looks like and I can tell it from a bad one. And I understand the components that go into it. I could describe the technicalities to you in almost infinitely parsed detail.

But that isn't the same as understanding how it's done. Understanding how the decision is made, how the movement of the bowler before he releases changes my balance and intent, how the weight is transferred, how the texture and intensity of my grip on the bat alters, how the hundred different muscles in my core interact to subtly transfer the power from legs to hands, how the exact balance and weight of *this* bat is accounted and adjusted for, or how what I have learned about the pace and bounce of *this* pitch, so different from so many of the surfaces on which I have hit balls, is built into the calculation, or how what I see in the final milliseconds before contact adjusts the last impulses I send to the blade of the bat. If you can explain that to me, then you know a good deal more about cricket than I do.

I know the properties of a good shot. And I can give you an impressionistic sense of what it looks like. But that is not the same as understanding how it's done. No more than knowing exactly what the *Moonlight Sonata* sounds like enables you to play it.

Let's say you bowl me two balls and I hit one well and one badly. I can describe, retrospectively, the difference. But I don't actually understand *why* I hit one badly. If I *did*, I wouldn't have fluffed it.

So my career, my whole future, is dependent on a process I can neither understand nor control, on skills I have to trust despite their inherent untrustworthiness. I hand over control of my destiny to agents I don't command because, if I don't do so, failure is swift and inevitable.

I have given up trying to really understand my technique. I go out and I hit balls, as well as I can in that moment.

And that's it.

But Darwin suggests that's OK.

Sunday 3.42 p.m.

Australia	348 and 405 for 7 dec
England	179 and 180 for 2 (68 overs)

We are cheered all the way through the Long Room and up the stairs, and there is a roar from inside as we come through the dressing-room door at tea. We are greeted with back slaps and hugs and, even better than that, with the news that the radar is showing rain arriving some time in the next hour or so.

We are within touching distance of going into the last day with a fighting chance of retaining the Ashes. One more good hour and we are back in the series.

*

Jabba is peering morosely at his iPhone. 'Do you ever feel that the happier someone's Facebook page looks, the more likely you are to hear one day that they've thrown themselves under a train?'

'Come on now, Jabba, back to work – if you can call it that. We know you just sit at the back of the Press Box playing Angry Birds all day.'

'Those little green pigs aren't going to kill themselves, you know.'

'Bottle of red and your iPhone and you're set for the evening session.'

'You don't booze on the job, do you, Jabba?'

The Test

'If you can suggest a better way for me to drink myself into an early grave, then I'd love to hear it. Anyway, do you blame me, having to put up with that lot?'

'You old alky!'

'You think *I* drink? Some of them make me look like a Methodist.' He nods in the direction of the Press Box. 'One of them got to the point where spirits weren't strong enough for him, so he switched to meths. It got so bad he was drinking a litre of brake fluid a day.'

'Jeeesus!'

'He's all right, though: he can stop whenever he wants.'

The groans echo round the room.

'So why doesn't he?'

'Fuck's sake, Tayls!'

'What?' he asks, looking bemused. 'Ooh . . .'

★

'Like they say, "It's not the thingy that gets you it's the . . . wotsname."'

'Thanks Tayls, profound and insightful as ever. Always leave them wanting less, eh?'

I leave them teasing him, and pop to the loo. When I come back, the dressing room is in uproar. Grub is bent over, flush-faced, howling with laughter. Oak is wiping tears from his cheeks.

Tayls has a patient, put-upon look. He shrugs and rolls his eyes at me.

'Having fun then, fellas?'

I turn from Grub, who can't answer, to Jabba, who is smirking like a schoolboy. *What's going on, Jabba?*

'Tayls has, once more, been demonstrating his extraordin-ary erudition, as only he can' he drawls.

He drops easily into Grub's Geordie accent. 'Here's one, Tayls. "What's a tangerine?"'

He switches to Tayls's Home Counties drawl. '"Oh, you know,"' and he makes a bouncing-up-and-down motion. '"What kids jump on in the garden."'

He waves his hand in despair, 'There were others.'

'I've got one, I've got one,' Grub pipes up. 'Which countries did we fight against in the Second World War, Tayls?'

Tayls sighs good-naturedly, then shrugs to indicate he has no idea, 'I'm gonna say . . . Vietnam?'

Behind us Jabba chokes on his coffee.

'You're supposed to drink it, not inhale it, Jab.'

'Oh god,' he groans in despair.

Tayls looks over at him, 'Oh right, were they on our side?'

'See,' says Grub, 'bordering on genius. If he knew what he was saying, he'd be the funniest man I'd ever met.'

I shrug, 'Frankly I'm just happy that he's awake and padded up.'

On the TV, the highlights of the India versus Sri Lanka ODI are playing. Tayls glances up at the screen and tries to change the subject. 'They have some odd sponsors, don't they, Sri Lanka? I mean, who are Dilmah anyway? Some random mobile-phone company?'

'Nah man,' says Grub, 'they make tea . . .'

He freezes, horror on his face, unable to believe what he's just allowed to happen.

But Tayls is already off and running, arms aloft, on a slow-motion victory lap of the dressing room, delightedly collecting high-fives as he goes.

Grub slumps backwards into his seat, lifts his arms and drops them into his lap in a whole-body shrug of abjection.

The Test

'Come on then,' says Tayls, from across the room. He has stopped by the kettle and is motioning towards it. Grub levers himself upright and heads over to take his medicine. The orders come ringing in from all corners of the dressing room.

Rope-a-dope, or just a lucky punch on the break?
We'll never know.
I reach for my thigh pad.
Right then, Mac. Back to work.

As I walk out of the door, I see them moving back to their positions. An old dressing-room superstition, this one, endemic in professional cricket. If it's going well in the middle, you stay where you are. When a long partnership is in progress, everyone has to stay put.

Grub for example, is going back to lie on the patch of floor under the window. He was there when we started this morning, so that's where he has to spend the day.

He can't see the match – or even the TV – from where he is, so relies entirely on the noise of the crowd and the others to let him know what is going on. 'Most relaxed I've ever been with you batting,' he told me over tea.

Sunday 4.37 p.m.

Australia	348 and 405 for 7 dec
England	179 and 207 for 2 (75 overs)

We are both approaching our centuries now. I don't say a word about it to Casey. Just keep plugging the same lines I've been trotting out all day. Breaking it down into ten-minute chunks, and the individual overs and balls within them.

He knows he's on 98, I know he's on 98. I would love him to get his hundred. *He bloody deserves it.* But it's not why we're here. Let's keep focused on the job at hand.

'Right, ten more minutes to drinks. Let's just get that far. Keep going, mate.' We punch gloves.

The next over passes without incident. A single off the last ball takes him to 99 and keeps him on strike for the start of the next over.

He looks tense. I try to relax him, joking about one of the opposition as we chat between overs, but he can't even raise a smile in response.

The Aussie captain is playing on his nerves, bringing all the fielders in to save one, and taking forever about it. Then, just as the bowler starts to run-up, he stops him to make another minor adjustment. Eventually the bowler runs in, and it is clear from the first two balls that they have adjusted tactics to use Casey's score against him.

Both balls are wide, length balls. Easy leaves, playing into our hands in trying to save the match, but hard to score off safely. Casey is going to have to take an unnecessary risk, play a shot he shouldn't play to get to his hundred.

He leaves the first and, after starting to flirt with it, the second as well. The third he flails at wildly. It's a panicky shot, completely unlike anything he has done for the last four hours. Luckily, he misses the ball by a distance; the umpire turns and signals it as wide. The slips gasp at the play-and-miss, and shout their encouragement to the bowler.

I walk down to talk to Casey.

'Easy, mate. No rush here. Just bat, let the score take care of itself.'

'Yeh . . . I know,' he says, shaking his head, 'shit shot!'

'Look, he hasn't got much margin for error, bowling out there. He'll miss his length eventually. Be patient. Wait for the right ball. And when you get it . . .' I grin. '. . . Smash it.'

We go back to our positions. Casey leaves the next three balls. Good leaves, too. Balanced, relaxed and disdainful, he watches the ball go past without any hint of interest.

Good lad. Just wait, it'll come.

And it does. The next ball is too short, dragged down, inviting the cut shot. Casey pounces, climbs into it for all he is worth, cutting it up and over the ring fielders, one bounce and it thuds into the boundary boards in front of the Mound Stand.

He turns, both arms raised towards the dressing room, and punches the air. Then trots down the wicket and grabs me in a bear hug, nearly lifting me off the ground.

The crowd are on their feet, and the ovation goes on and on, Casey turning slowly around, bat raised, basking in their adulation. The thirty-thousand-throated roar casts him in bronze, statuesque against a shaft of evening light.

Century on debut, what about that? Bloody brilliant, lad.

Eventually, the applause subsides and we go back to our ends.

I turn the next ball off my hip; it goes finer than I intended, and fine leg makes a mess of his sliding stop, kicking the ball into the ropes by mistake. That takes me to 98.

The sky behind the pavilion is getting darker and darker, and with the new ball due soon, I'm keen to get off the pitch with our wickets still intact. Facing a new ball in the dark with a whole day's batting in our legs is going to be no fun at all.

Come on, Mac, keep your mind in the game here. One ball at a time.

The next ball squirts off my outside edge, bounces short of second slip and runs away to third man off his fingertips. The other slips turn to give chase. *Could be two here!*

I set off, but I can barely get my exhausted limbs going. With fresh legs and working knees this is an easy two, but my knee explodes in pain as I turn and, looking up, I realise I'm not going to make it. Then I see with horror that Casey is halfway back. Eager to get me to a hundred he has turned for the second without looking, and is sprinting back towards me. *If I send him back he'll never make it.*

As always, there is a split second to make the decision, and it has been made and I am moving before I know what I've decided. I'm running. As if in a nightmare, my legs refusing to work properly, the throw already coming in, arriving at the stumps with me well short.

The Test

I'm not going to make it. I'm going to be out by two yards.

But it bounces awkwardly, just in front of the keeper, who doesn't gather it cleanly. I throw myself full-length, straining forward with the tip of my bat for the crease. It's an ugly sprawl. My head whiplashes forward, hits the ground hard, the visor smashing into my face. *But, I'm safe!*

I lie on the ground. Not entirely sure that I can get up. But then Casey is there, hauling me to my feet, and is hugging me for the second time in ten minutes.

I lift my bat to the dressing room; even from here I can see that Reg the attendant has got himself right in the middle of the applauding group on the balcony. *Made sure you turned up now, didn't you Reg? Get yourself on the telly.* It's the first time I've seen him all day.

I turn, taking in the whole ground. Again, I have that feeling that I am standing at the centre of the world. I lift my bat to each corner and, finally, to Dad. He lifts both hands above his head in reply, fists clenched.

*

'Bloody dark out here, Tony.'

'We'll take a light-meter reading at the end of the over,' replies the umpire.

'Do you think you'll be able to see it?' I ask. He smiles back.

We are three overs into the new ball. The floodlights are on, the sky is black, and there are the first spots of rain in the air. We can see it raining hard in the distance behind the pavilion.

It's bloody difficult out here now. I've barely put bat on ball in the last ten minutes, and I've been out here all day. If we lose a wicket, then the new batsman is really going to struggle.

I've been getting into the umpires for the last fifteen minutes about the light. But so have the Aussies, of course, who are desperate to stay out here and do us some damage before the rain ends play for the day.

The next ball climbs steeply off a length, catches Casey on the gloves and drops into the leg-side. McKenzie, under the lid at short leg, dives forward and scoops the ball up. The Aussies appeal delightedly, convinced that it's out. McKenzie leaps to his feet and roars into Casey's distraught face from two feet away, and points him back to the dressing room before running to hug his teammates.

Hang on, that didn't look right.

Casey clearly doesn't think so either. He looks at me, I motion for him to stay where he is. There was more than a suspicion that the ball bounced.

The umpires confer and then refer it upstairs to the TV umpire. The big screen starts showing replays of the catch. It looks dubious, to say the least.

'You cheating little fucker.' Casey has seen a review on the big screen, and, convinced that the ball has bounced, he has gone to confront McKenzie. Now they are nose to nose, spitting insults at each other. Half the fielding team crowd in to add their weight to the fight.

Oh God, not again.

I hurry over, grab Casey by the arm and tug him away from the scrap. The Aussie captain is doing the same to McKenzie. The pair are still firing obscenities back and forth. The umpires arrive and separate the two sides, pushing us apart and putting some distance between us.

After a few moments things calm down a bit. We all go back to staring at the big screen. The replays are still running.

Then it switches to the 'Decision Pending' sign. It spins and the decision flashes up on to the screen: 'OUT'.

The crowd gasps in dismay. I am stunned. I know these things are always open to interpretation, and you tend to see what you want to see, but I was convinced that they would give that Not Out.

Casey swears under his breath and stares at me in astonishment.

I shrug. 'Bad luck, mate.'

The fielders are delighted, high-fiving and jeering at Casey as he turns to walk off the field.

And now, five minutes too late, the rain finally arrives. The sky darkens further, and by the time Tayls has got to the boundary rope, it has strengthened into a steady downpour.

The umpires pull up the stumps, and the ground staff race the covers on to the pitch, the strengthening wind tugging at the edges.

Disappointing end, but an unbelievable day from where we were.

I turn and look up at the media centre, where the lights are bright against the gathering gloom. *Take that, you smug pricks. Not dead yet, eh?*

I suddenly have one of my vertigo moments, and I have to turn and stamp off towards the pavilion to stop myself signalling in their direction. In fact, my arm has already started its swing up into an obscene gesture before I come to my senses and turn my back instead.

Not cool, Mac. Not cool at all, that was way too close.

★

'Well done, Mac. You managed nearly a whole day during which almost nothing happened.'

'Just another thrilling day at the Test match.'

'*Cricket is a game which the English, not being a spiritual people, have invented to give themselves some conception of eternity.*'

I'm sure he's quoting someone, but I don't recognise it.

'Thanks, Jabba. Keeping my feet on the ground as always.'

'No, it was remarkable. It was like watching grass grow, but with people in the way.'

'Well, we can all come back and do it again tomorrow.'

'Hurrah. Also, you should know that SKY have found another camera angle. It shows the ball clearly bounced. Do you want to tell Casey, or shall I?'

Sunday 5.45 p.m.

Jabba is in the corner. He is briefing Casey ahead of his press interviews. The big man looks a bit worried, and I can understand why; Casey is odds-on to say at least one thing that will cause Jabba a long night's work.

'You're pleased with the way you played, but we've still got a long way to go in the match etc., etc. They'll want you to comment on the decision. Don't. They'll want to make something of it. Don't criticise the umpires, don't complain. If you do, we'll just be whingeing Poms. They get a free headline, we look like sore losers. They'll want to talk about selection for the winter tour . . .'

This is a variation on Jabba's standard briefing to new players. You're talking to the public, not to the press. Don't complain, don't feel sorry for yourself. A nurse getting off a twelve-hour shift isn't going to feel sympathy for you over your five-star hotel and your business-class flights, even if you did get a rough decision.

'Can I tell them what I think about McKenzie?' I think he's joking, but it's not always easy to tell. Jabba is about to reply, but I come in on this one.

'Don't say anything in the press about a fellow professional that you wouldn't be happy to say to his face and, more importantly, to his family.

'They'll see it, they'll read it. If you'd be happy to slag him off to his kids, and his parents and his wife, then go ahead. But once it's out there, it's out there. You can't un-say it.'

He grins. 'Don't worry. I'll behave.'

I nod and walk away, more concerned rather than less.

Later, I watch his interview. He does well.

Needless to say, the media have flipped effortlessly through 180 degrees. They are now indulging themselves in a full-scale deification of Casey. He is being fawningly interviewed by the very commentator who ripped him to shreds yesterday.

'A lot of people were saying yesterday that they didn't think you were up to it . . .'

Yeh, you! You disingenuous prick.

Sunday 6.45 p.m.

I get the roomie to bring in a cooler full of beers for the boys, and we sit together for half an hour chatting and laughing. When Casey is back from doing the press and we are all together, I stand up and call for quiet.

'Well, fellas, you've heard this before. But it's not about how many times you get knocked down; it's about how many times you get back up.' I look around the room at smiling faces. *God, it feels like a while since we've been happy in here.*

'We didn't win anything today. And we've still got a lot of work to do tomorrow to get anything out of this game.

'But, we did get back up off the canvas, and for the first time in this match we landed some punches of our own.

'They came here today to collect the Ashes. Now, they're tired, and sore, and no closer to winning than they were this morning. I don't know what'll happen tomorrow, but I'd much rather be in this dressing room than theirs—'

'Quite right. Theirs is full of wankers,' Grub chips in.

I raise my bottle of water amidst the laughter. 'They were saying this morning that we'd sent a boy to do a man's job.'

There are snorts from the room. Someone reaches over and slaps Casey on the back. 'Now they're saying: if you're old enough you're good enough.

'Casey, you may be prettier than any of Grub's girlfriends – ' they laugh – 'and we may not be able to understand a word you say. But today you showed you were the real deal, and that this – ' the wave of my arm takes in the dressing room, the ground, and the Test arena in general – 'is where you belong. That was pure class, mate.'

I lift the bottle higher. 'To Casey . . . and the first of many!' The room roars its agreement. I sip my water.

'Now, Tayls. If you can somehow contrive to break your recent habit and be awake at the start of play tomorrow, then you and I have got a job to do. Enjoy the evening, gents. Tomorrow we retain the Ashes.'

That's all I've got. I am completely spent and my knee is killing me, and I fall back into my chair.

Casey wanders over and sits next me. 'Thanks for that.'

'You're welcome,' I say, clinking my bottle of water against his beer.

'And thanks for . . . you nor . . .' he nods at the pitch, 'oot there. Couldn't 'a dun it we-art you.'

'*You* did it. I was just lucky to be there to watch.' He smiles at this. 'I meant it, you know. You're born for this . . . don't waste it.' I think he's going to bridle at this. He starts to, and then relaxes, tilts his head in acknowledgement instead.

'Can I ask . . . ? Why'd you pick me?' he asks eventually.

I nod past him. Rob's cap is hanging in his usual space. We brought it down with us, hung it there and left his space empty. 'It's *him* you have to thank.

234

'I went to see him in hospital before I drove down from Leeds. He was in a pretty bad way ... tubes ... drugs ... everything. I was halfway through asking him how he was, when he pulled his mask off and said, "*Thomas ... Casey Thomas.*"

'I said, "Are you sure? I mean, it's not an easy match to make your debut in. We've got other options, guys who've played a few Tests, who know what it's like out there." "Thomas," he says. "I've seen him play. He's the genuine article. He's your man."

'So I took that to the selectors. They would have gone for experience, but were frankly terrified of having to make the call. So they went with Rob.'

He snorts into his beer at the thought. 'How heavily drugged was he?'

'Very,' I laugh. 'But he was right, wasn't he, so let's not knock it.'

We are both staring up at the cap as if it is our missing captain.

'He *is* the real deal,' I say. 'You won't meet many better men. You can trust him; he won't let you down. He was ready to put his faith in you, after all.'

'*The substance of things hoped for, the evidence of things not seen?*' he says. I stare at him. I'm pretty sure my mouth has fallen open. He grins at my dumbfoundedness.

'How ... ?'

'I went to school, you know. No need to look like that.'

'Sorry, I didn't mean—'

'Nah, don't worry. Jus' kiddin'. I heard you yelling at Jabba the other day, didn't know what you were talking about, so I googled it on my phone.'

'It's Hebrews 11:1.'

'If you says so. And sorry for . . . you know . . . getting het up out there. You must think I have a scrap a match. I don't.'

'Well at least you didn't hit me this time, I suppose. Remember, though, you've got a long rest of your life to live.' I pause, searching for a way of putting the thought into words. 'The afterglow of what you do now colours the whole of the rest of your life. Years of meeting friends of friends, of standing on touchlines watching your kids play, of turning up to job interviews and speaking at club dinners. What you do now, you live with for ever. And sometimes, one moment can define a career. One moment of brilliance, one moment of ignominy.'

He seems to accept this, nods soberly. Then a thought occurs to him and he grins.

'Hey, you realise that I *could* argue I haven't actually been out in Test cricket yet,' he laughs.

'It's a fair point, actually.'

My phone beeps. I check the screen.

Have you got time to buy your old man a drink?

'You came', I say.

'I came.' We hug. 'Well batted, Son.'

'Thanks, Dad.'

And there, that simply, we are past something.

Something that's been in the way for two years. I couldn't tell you what it was, can't put it into words. But it's been there ever since Mum passed away. And now it isn't.

We sit down.

I take a deep breath, and nearly slide off the chair.

'God, I'm knackered!' I groan.

'You look done in! I shouldn't be keeping you from your bed.' He half rises from his chair.

'No, don't worry. It's great to see you. I've got to eat anyway. They do food here, don't they; do you want to grab a bite?'

'I'll get some menus.' He gets up and crosses to the bar and back again.

'Oh, never get old, James,' he sighs when he comes back, tossing the menus on to the table. 'I just saw an old man across the room, and it took me ten seconds to realise it was a mirror.'

I smile in sympathy.

'It happens *whenever* I see myself these days. The face in

the mirror looks wrong, like I've put on someone else's clothes,' he says wonderingly.

He reaches into his bag and slides an envelope across the table. I open it and pull out a photograph. Mum and Dad, fresh out of university and impossibly young, are arm in arm, grinning in the Cannes sunshine. I remember it from twenty years ago, when it hung on the wall at home.

'I found it in the move, remembered you'd always liked it.' He shakes his head wonderingly at the young version of himself. 'All those things that seemed so important. Hard to believe, that they're gone . . . that they weren't.' He smiles to take the sting out of his words. 'Suddenly my life feels like a box of old marking.'

He laughs at this, and I do too, then he looks down at the menu to break the moment.

'Right, what are you going to have?'

After we've placed our orders, he nods down at my leg. 'How's the knee?'

I screw my face up and shake my head slightly in reply.

'Will it last another day?'

'It's going to have to.'

'And the winter tours?'

I sigh. 'I don't know, Dad. Every time I think about it, my heart sinks. I honestly don't know how much I've got left in me.'

He smiles his sympathy. 'You'll know, I reckon. You'll know when.'

He is in a voluble mood. I think a couple of pints in hospitality may be responsible. I'm happy just to listen. I don't have the energy for much else anyway.

The Test

And at least someone has celebrated my ton properly.

'Amazing how life gets complicated without you realising,' he says. 'When I first started teaching, I didn't have much to do. Work was simple, my timetable was pretty light. I used to nap in the middle of the day and go out most nights. Term time was hardly any busier than the holidays.'

Sounds good, I could see myself as a teacher next.

'Then, slowly, I got busier and busier . . . picked up roles I was interested in, got flattered into taking on ones I wasn't . . . It's always much easier to take jobs on than to get rid of them . . . And suddenly the days weren't quite long enough. The To-Do List never got finished, just got longer.

'Then I married your mum, and you guys came along, and there was far more to do at home. No matter what I did, there just weren't enough hours in the day.

'There were times when I'd hide. Just close the door and stare at the wall.' He is grinning at himself. 'I stopped doing things I enjoyed because I knew I had too many other things I'd promised to do. I let life set around me like concrete.

'It's only now looking back that I sort of see what happens. As your reach grows, so do the number of things within your grasp. The more you do, the more opportunities you get. The more people you know, the more things are asked of you.

'First, it's just you. Then you have a house, and a car. Then a family, and another car, and a laundry list of responsibilities.

'If life was once about just doing the next obvious thing in front of you, suddenly it has become more complex, a labyrinth of Hydra-headed demands. Doors lead to doors, in a maze that multiplies to the point of exhaustion and beyond.'

'You're not making it sound much fun,' I say, grinning.

He laughs.

'We are all broken vessels, trying to carry too much water,' I offer. 'Says Jabba anyway. That one and: Life is trying to pick out a tune we don't know on a broken piano.'

'He sounds a barrel of laughs too.'

'He's more fun than I'm making him out to be.'

But I also realise that what he is describing is different. I am often busy, and occasionally short of time. But my problem isn't *too many* ties, but not enough. I am never in one place long enough for my routines to calcify in the way he is describing.

'I don't know. It's different for me. Sometimes I wonder if I did ever actually grow up. I changed, definitely. I got older. I got slower. But, I've got school friends who save lives every day; others who run businesses and manage dozens of people; two who've seen combat in Iraq and Afghanistan . . . Whereas I . . . hit a ball with a stick.'

'You hit it pretty well.'

'I do, I generally hit it pretty well. But, I'm a kid. I'm a thirty-three-year-old kid.'

'Aye, lad. But you'll do. You'll do.'

★

He never taught me, or coached me, but I did do his Creative Writing course when I was in the Lower Sixth.

I can still see him at the introductory session, the first time I had been in front of him as a student.

It is a November evening. He hurries through the door five minutes late, drops into his chair, swings his feet up on to the desk and sweeps his eyes around the dozen or so would-be writers scattered around the room.

He looks more rugby coach than poet, having come straight from the training pitch in his kit. Mud is drying on his calves in the warmth of the classroom, and his dirt-framed fingernails are tapping rhythmically on the tattered green leather of his desk. He stares at each of us in turn.

There is some nervous shuffling from behind me, but otherwise silence.

He stops tapping, lets the pause lengthen theatrically, and then surges back to his feet and leans forward, both hands on his desk top.

'Gentlemen . . . if I may,' he begins slowly, faux-respect-fully, the Border Scots, usually a gentle hint in his voice, more pronounced than usual, adding edge and heft to his words '. . . we are here to an end . . .

'So that when we wind on twenty years:
To your two-hour commute to the job that you hate,
And to the grey face in the mirror, three stone heavier
And older than you could ever believe,
To the four weeks of holiday a year you daren't take
And to the one weekend in three with your kids,
That *you* circle in the diary, and *they* hate . . .'

He is prowling now, slow and steady, about the classroom, the rhythm of his movements in time with the lines, powerful and mesmeric.

'To the life, in short, that you've aimed yourself at,
Like an arrow, since your first Prep School blazer.'

He stops at the back of the room, and stands staring out of the window.

Rain is starting to fall on the glass. We can hear it drumming on the roof in the sudden quiet. Outside, the heavy sky has drained the colour from the world in a premature dusk.

'*Gentlemen . . .*' he turns back to us and starts to move again '. . . this is our task.

'We are here to listen;
to ourselves, to each other
And to the dead faces behind words.
We are here to stare at the wall
and see through it,
Past the shade and the shadows, to light.
We are here to sow wild flowers amidst the corn,
To rediscover the stoniness of the stone
To stand on the shoulders of giants as
we find the stillness between breaths,

'To learn how to squeeze, from books,
    And from life its very self, the passion to live.

'We are here to throw ourselves at windmills
    knowing that we can only win by losing.

    'Gentlemen . . .' Now he is back at the front of the room, arms folded, smiling, '. . . we are here to write.'

The hair on the back of my neck is standing up.

'Who wrote that?' I ask him later that evening, after we got home.

'What?'

'The poem you quoted at the start.'

'I did.'

'Thought so,' I nod. 'It was good.' I would happily gush about it, but I know he will be far happier with a simple affirmation than with more fulsome praise.

Our food arrives. I've ordered half a chicken and chips. The moment I take a bite I realise I am absolutely famished. I demolish the rest without saying a word.

'You look like you needed that!'

'You have no idea.'

'So, how is it captaining a Test team?'

'Not as easy as it might look!'

'No, I can imagine.'

'In the words of Mike Tyson, "Everyone's got a plan until they get punched in the mouth".'

'Have you spoken to Stocksy?'

'No, but I've been channelling him,' I laugh. 'Trotting out pretty much everything he ever told me.'

*

Plates cleared, we sit and nurse a Diet Coke each, watching the pub slowly fill up.

'Have you seen Beth and the kids recently?' He says it carefully, like someone probing a sore tooth.

'Couple of weeks ago. Feels longer.'

He nods sympathetically. I look for the hint of judgement behind his eyes, but it isn't there, just shared pain.

'Joyce was right,' he mutters, almost to himself. 'Absence is the highest form of presence.

'The loved ones we're away from . . .' He gazes down at the table, continues as if he is explaining to both of us, 'the ones we feel like an ache, are ever present, in a way that they actually aren't when they're still part of our lives.'

The pub chatters around us. He looks up.

'It's strange, you know . . . there can eventually be a sort of freedom in it . . .' and I know that now he is talking about Mum, '. . . born of the terrible.

'The worst thing happens, and yet suddenly somehow you're still alive. The sun comes up. The world carries on.

'And you think, what on earth is there to fear in the mundane? Once you've been to those depths, the day-to-day can't touch you. The grip of all your petty inhibitions loses any force.'

We chat on for a while, until my eyes start to droop mid-sentence, and I have to admit defeat.

When we hug goodnight it takes a while. He feels smaller in my arms than I remember. I don't want to let go.

Eventually I step back.

'Night, Dad.'

'Night, Son.'

Two weeks ago

The brightest sun casts the darkest shadows.

I am dropping the kids off at Beth's, my mind already turning half guiltily to tomorrow's match.

I stand on the pavement and watch them run up the path.

Sam is inside already, his farewell called over his shoulder.

Emily's little feet are trotting towards Beth.

The teddy bear that I weakened about, gave in, and bought for her, dangles forgotten in my hand. And suddenly the ground feels unsteady beneath me.

Then she turns.

Trots back.

Hugs me.

'Bye, Dada.'

'Bye, little one. See you soon.'

Well, then: still hero to this small heart.

I turn to leave, but Beth calls out after me.

'Hey, McCall!' and then, as I look back, 'Good luck tomorrow.'

I nod thanks, and go back to the car. I wait for the front

245

door to close before I start the engine, and then a minute or two more before I pull away.

I'm finding it hard to breathe.

Later, as the dark road insinuates itself between them and me, I can feel my sense of them evaporating.

I lose them when I'm away.

I forget the way they smell, the feel of their tiny limbs when I hug them. Being away from them isn't something that gets easier with time, only ever harder. The pain doesn't ease. The ache doesn't fade. It sharpens.

The feeling of separation is visceral. Knowing they are out there in the world somewhere, going to school, laughing and playing, or falling, crying and looking for you.

The highest form of presence.

You can give it the slip on a busy day. With enough distraction, you can forget it for hours at a time. But the aching hole just waits for you as you go about your business.

Then you turn a corner, and a child is playing, and their smile is a punch to your stomach.

Like trying to stare at the sun: it is too bright, too painful.

The brightest sun casts the darkest shadows.

I look at the six steps up to the front of the hotel. I'm so woozy with fatigue, they look almost cliff-like, and halfway up, my legs nearly give way. *Come on Mac, get it together.*

In the lobby, Tayls is chatting to his parents. I would go and say hello, but the mental text messages from my duvet are getting more and more insistent, so I raise a hand in greeting and keep walking. They nod back, Dad scruffily posh and affable, South African-born Mum all Farrow-and-Ball hair and condescension.

I cross to the lifts where I bump into, almost literally, a distinctly worse-for-wear team media manager. Eyes unfocused, he is gently bouncing off the walls like a vast, heavyweight moth.

'Jabba,' I grunt in greeting.

He looks in the direction of my voice, pulling himself upright with comic care.

'Mac . . . evening . . .' he mumbles.

I reach past him to press the lift button, something he seems to have neglected to do.

Jabba in his cups is an unlovely sight, and an unpredictable experience. Something seems to occur to him and he lifts a finger, as if he is about to make an important point.

'There is always . . .' he starts, then pauses, lost in thought for a while, before continuing ponderously, 'No . . . got it . . . There is always some madness in love. But there is also always some reason in madness.'

'It's too late for Nietzsche, Jabba. Why don't we get you to bed, eh?'

The lift doors open and I step inside.

'Never too late . . . never too late . . .' he shakes his head sombrely and follows me. Mozart's 'Eine kleine Nachtmusik' tinkles at us as the lift sets off.

'We are supposed to live in the moment, to avoid . . .' he stops again, grasping for something. 'All life is *dukkha*, suffering . . . suffering is caused by attachment . . . craving and aversion . . .'

'Glad those months in the monastery weren't wasted, Jab.' *I am way too tired for this.*

'The man who can avoid attachment, who doesn't care what others think, becomes . . . *Übermensch* . . . a Superman.'

The lift doors open at my floor and I step out.

'But if we *can* leave our fears behind, remain untouched, if all means nothing . . . then . . . are we not left with nothing but the end?'

Jabba is now standing on the threshold, with the lift doors bumping gently against him. He doesn't seem to notice them as he warms to his theme. 'If we *were* to let go of our failings, our weaknesses, what then is there to shield us from the full glare of our mortality?' He hiccups extravagantly. 'Is it not our fears . . . our loves . . . our petty vanities . . . that obscure the path enough to make it worth walking? Without them . . . without them, aren't we just left with . . . one long trudge . . . towards cold . . . oblivion?'

It's never a great idea to debate with a drunk Jabba, and I am desperate to get to my bed.

'You've never been overly encumbered by hope, Jabba, but this is bleak even for you. Maybe this is a discussion we should have in the morning.'

'It always seems darkest . . . just before it goes totally black!' he says glumly.

'More Nietzsche?'

'No . . . Charlie Brown,' he says with a twisted grin.

OK, you got me.

'So . . .' He is declaiming now '. . . I will hold close my shortcomings. A . . . shield . . . against the darkness.'

'Mixing your metaphors a little there, Jab – what room are you in, anyway?'

'Don't know. I was just trying to remember when you came along.'

Brilliant.

I pull out my phone and ring our team manager.

'Sorry to bother you, Paul. Do you happen to know which room Jabba's in? 1351 . . . great, thanks, night.'

'Come on then, big fella, back in the lift.'

I shoo him back inside, and press the button for his floor.

'You still haven't given me an answer,' he says grumpily.

'Major Allison Digby Tatham-Warter.'

'What?'

'That's my answer.'

'Allison who?' he grumbles.

'Tatham-Warter, Second Parachute Battalion, took the bridge at Arnhem.' The doors open and we step back out of the lift. 'Used to go into battle armed only with an umbrella.'

Jabba scowls at this, as he walks unsteadily down the corridor next to me.

'’n umbrella?'

I nod. 'An umbrella. His friends would say to him, "What will you do if you end up in a firefight?"'

'And what did he say?'

'"Ah," he'd reply ". . . but what will *you* do if it rains?"'

We arrive at Jabba's door, and after a couple of attempts he manages to open it.

He nods as if conceding the point, '*Touché, touché*.'

'Night, Jabba.'

'Night, Mac.'

The door swings shut between us.

Swaying with fatigue, I turn and trudge back towards the lifts.

I am sliding, sideways, into the past.

He is waiting. Sunlit, and smiling.

I am throwing ball after ball, slow, underarm, searching for the middle of his bat. Grinning at each missed shot, encouraging, cajoling. He is alternately giggling and grunting in frustration. Sulkily comic as he stamps his foot after missing another one.

Then suddenly, surprising himself, he middles one precise and true. Nailed through the centre of its being, it shoots past me, crisp as the first bite of an apple, seam stunned still by the perfection of the contact. His mouth shapes an O of surprise and wonder.

That's it. There it is:

The Moment.

The one that grabs us all. The one that hooks us in, after the litany of failed or flawed attempts, of hacks and hoicks, misses, edges, and the ones that hit the toe of the bat and jar the fingers.

The unlooked-for joy of that first sweet impact.

The one that will keep us coming back, because it will always be there, on the very edge of our furthest reach.

I drift back into darkness.

And I'm six again.

Dad is bowling to me, again and again, trying to coax the ball on to the middle of my bat.

And circles are turning,

wheels spinning,

forward and forward and forward

Down into the dark.

Love's austere and lonely offices.

That strange knowing, that strangeness of knowing...

There are ten of us by the river.

We walk until we find her favourite spot. Then Dad leads us down to the edge of the water and turns to face us.

'Thank you all for coming,' he says, and then pauses to steady himself, looks down at the urn in his hands.

Even before he starts, I know exactly what he is going to say. We haven't discussed it, but now we are here it is obvious.

'*The Sunlight on the garden*
Hardens and grows cold
We cannot cage the minute
Within its nets of gold . . .'

Louis MacNeice's masterpiece was always Mum's favourite. She insisted on its bittersweet perfection as one of the readings at their wedding. It is the one poem I learned from her, and not from him.

'*When all is told*
We cannot beg for pardon.'

I gaze at my father, upright and still in his quiet dignity, and it is as if I am seeing him anew: the clean precision of his shirt and tie, the greying hair, now neatly combed into submission.

His voice is strong, and clear. There is a half-smile on his lips. There is sadness there, but something far more powerful gleaming underneath its shade. His eyes shine.

'. . . *And soon, my friend*
We shall have no time for dances . . .'

I came prepared to support him if need be. Confident that I would be OK, I was ready for him not to be.

But, all of a sudden, I find myself falling apart, unmanned by his stoicism.

Tears are streaming down my cheeks and the back of my throat is a clenching ache. I close my eyes and feel my face crumple.

Images of Mum swim up, one after another. I hear a high keening from nearby, that cuts off only when I realise it is coming from me.

'. . . *The sky was good for flying*
Defying the church bells . . .'

I feel an arm around my shoulders, and the smell of her tells me that it is Beth who has reached out to try and comfort me. I turn my head into her chest, and she squeezes me close. Her hair falls across my neck. She murmurs gently, and I can tell she is weeping too.

In the background, MacNiece is turning full circle as Dad approaches the final stanza.

'. . . *And every evil iron*
Siren and what it tells:
The earth compels,
We are dying, Egypt, dying.'

The line Shakespeare wrote for Cleopatra hits me as if I'd never heard it before. I fight back sob after sob. My chest is a sucking hole.

The Test

'*And not expecting pardon*
Hardened in heart anew
But glad to have sat under
Thunder and rain with you,
And grateful too
For sunlight on the garden.'

I force my eyes open. Dad is still standing there, smiling at me with his dreadful calm.

It's OK, his eyes are telling me, *it's all OK.*

Then he turns and scatters the ashes from the urn into the river.

And the blackness in my chest rises like a howl.

DAY FIVE

For all that international cricket is often a treadmill, the really big days are defined by pressure.

There is an Olympic sprint coach in the United States who will only work with you if you are a born-again Christian. Not through religious fervour, but from a purely practical point of view. He genuinely believes it makes you run faster if you have faith that God is on your side.

There are days when I can understand what he means. The appeal of handing over the doubt and responsibility to a higher power, of being able to let go of the pressure of your performance and trust an outside agency to take care of things is very appealing.

There are days, the big days, where the nerves never quite leave me. They are a bass note to the tune of my thoughts and emotions from the moment I wake up. When I am with people, or actively doing something, I don't find them so bad. But in the moments on my own they can start to swamp me, threaten to pull me down into panic and nausea.

It is Bank Holiday Monday, so the streets are eerily empty as I drive from the hotel to the ground, past tree-muffled squares and white-stone façades, built just for summer mornings like this.

I roll down Portland Place and into Regent's Park. The sun is shining, and the park belongs to joggers and cyclists, sweating their way through the crisp air.

I pull off the roundabout and am being held by the lights at the crossing when I see the line. It is 8.30 in the morning, and the queue is three abreast, all the way round the ground and back down the road as far as I can see in the direction of St John's Wood tube station.

The regular crowd at Lord's is a peculiar animal, unlike any other Test crowd in England. Demure, slightly distracted. They are here to see old friends, and to catch up. To drink and picnic. To be seen. They were at Henley, and Ascot. They've grabbed a week or two away in the Maldives, and now they are here to spend a last weekend with Charlie and a couple of his chums at the cricket before they drop him back at school for the start of the Michaelmas Term. Ooh look, a wicket – better applaud politely; which team are batting again?

There are expensive seats that are never sat in, whose would-be inhabitants sit drinking in the champagne tents with old school friends all day and don't see a ball bowled.

Today though, it is *very* different.

These are another type of fan. They've dug themselves out of bed in the early hours of a Bank Holiday and queued since dawn, with their sandwiches and their flasks, sat in their seats for nearly two hours before the start of play. They are here to live every ball. Win, lose or draw, they are here because they would be absolutely nowhere else.

They are the middle Sunday at Wimbledon fans, the away

terrace at the other end of the country fans. And by God they are going to make sure we know they're here.

From the start of their warm-up, the Australians are in no doubt – whatever it felt like on the other days – that today they are definitely the *away* team. The pantomime villains in their side are booed from the second their feet hit the grass.

And from the moment play starts, the intensity is like nothing I've ever experienced. Every leave is clapped, every forward defensive shot cheered. Every unsuccessful appeal howled at with derision. The boundary fielders have that fixed, staring-straight-ahead look that says, clear as day, that they are getting a verbal battering from the front rows of the stands behind.

Monday, 9.10 a.m.

Grub is peering meditatively at two different pairs of socks. He looks worried.

'What's the matter?'

'I'm not sure which is which.'

'What do you mean?'

'Well, that stain looks right, but I dinna think they were so worn around the toes.'

'Grub, what are you talking about?'

'Me lucky socks.'

'Right ...'

'Am not sure which they are. I always keep track of 'em, but they came back from the laundry and Reg's got 'em mixed in with the others.'

Grub has a pair of socks in which he has scored three Test hundreds. They are now barely recognisable as socks, but he still wears them on every important occasion possible. If I'm honest, both these pairs look much too new.

'What am I gonna do?' He looks gutted. 'Today of all days,' he adds bitterly.

'You know, Grub, it's entirely possible that our success or

failure doesn't hinge on which socks you wear. I'm just throwing that out there.'

He glares at me, then goes back to staring at his socks.

★

There are unwritten rules of 'neutral' ground at Test venues. The two teams spend a week or so rubbing up against each other. You share practice facilities, gyms, and often dining areas with the opposition.

Two players who have been facing off on the pitch could be queuing next to each other for lunch five minutes later. And so there is a sort of unofficial code of conduct for handling these moments.

When queuing for lunch in a shared dining room, the batting side will automatically step out of line and stand aside to let the fielders eat first.

If a wicket falls while you are on neutral ground, you won't see anyone celebrate, no matter how important the breakthrough. They may be jumping all over each other and punching the air in a dressing room just feet away, but if you're caught in the shared lunch room or gym, then cheering seems crass.

I slept in a bit, so after my hit in the nets I head upstairs to grab a quick breakfast. When I get there, the dining room is empty except for the Australian captain. I grab a bacon sandwich and a cup of tea and sit down opposite him.

I played a couple of seasons of county cricket with him for Middlesex, got to know him and his wife fairly well. I have always rated him as a genuinely good guy. Hard as teak, very much 'no quarter asked or given' on the field, but off it, relaxed, easy-going and self-effacing. He is firmly from the half of Oz that feels like a better, sunnier version of England thirty years ago, rather than the half that feels like white-trash America.

'Mac,' he nods.

'Morning, Steve,' I nod back, and put my plate down opposite him. 'How's Meg?'

He smiles, 'She's well, thanks. She was asking after you the other day. We're going to stay on for a couple of weeks' holiday at the end of the series. It would be good to grab some dinner and catch up . . . after all this.' He nods in the direction of the pitch.

That's odd. 'You're not playing the one-dayers?'

'No . . .' he pauses, seems to come to a decision, and then continues, 'Ah look, it's an open secret. I'm calling it a day after this one. Announcing after the match.'

'All cricket?'

He shakes his head. 'I'll play one more season for New South Wales, if the back'll take it.'

'Bad?'

'Fucked.'

I grimace sympathetically.

'Which is why I'd quite like you to stop this Lazarus act of yours, and let us all go home.' He grins at me. 'I don't want my last act in a Baggy Green to be letting the Poms hold on to the Ashes!'

'Well, we'll just have to see how we go, won't we then?' I smile back.

When I get back to the dressing room, I find our chief executive standing talking quietly to the head coach by the door to the balcony. With them is another guy in a suit. I know his face, but I couldn't tell you what he does. Most of the team are sitting around watching them. It is unnaturally quiet for the morning of a match and I am instantly annoyed: first, that they are there at all, and second, that they are clearly flattening the mood of the team.

Surely this could wait?

The third man steps forward to meet me, holding out his hand. 'Mac, Steven Wilson,' he introduces himself.

'Hi Steven, what's going on?'

He looks embarrassed. Behind him, Edwards the chief exec is looking furious, but stays silent. Wilson motions me closer, and lowering his voice says quietly, 'It's about Jabba. He was . . .' He pauses, clearly trying to work out exactly what to say.

'He was spotted in . . . indelicate circumstances with a young man of . . . negotiable virtue—'

'He means a fucking—' Edwards interjects.

'I know what he means,' I cut him off quietly. Sadly, this is not a complete surprise. But it couldn't have come at a worse time. *Oh Jabba, you bloody fool!*

'So what are we going to do for him?'

The looks on their faces are answer enough.

'I see. Where is he?'

Edwards jerks his head towards the back office. 'In there. I want him out of the building immediately!'

'The press have it, it is only a matter of time. We need to move quickly to limit the damage,' Wilson adds more mildly.

'No,' I shake my head. 'We're in the middle of a match. I want him here. He stays until we finish the game; you can sort this out after that.'

I'll be damned if I'm giving this prick the satisfaction of throwing Jabba out of the dressing room.

'Unacceptable, I won't have—'

'It's my team. He's part of it. He stays while we need him.' I look at our head coach for support. He looks as if he would be content for the ground to open up and swallow him, but eventually he nods his agreement. Edwards starts up again. 'Look . . .'

'You need to leave now. You can sort this out after the match,' I say firmly.

'Now—' he starts, and I snap. I jab a finger in the direction of the door.

'The sign on the door says "Admittance by permission of the Captain". You don't have it. You leave now, Mr Edwards. We've got a Test match to win here.' Wilson has already made his decision and is heading towards the door. Edwards tries to dig his heels in.

'Look, Mac, call me Johnny, and you don't need to be like—'

Something snaps. 'I'll call you what the fuck I like! Now get the hell out of my dressing room!' I shout.

Silence.

Edwards looks around the room, and now there is just a ring of hard eyes glaring him down. It is a difficult room to face down alone. At his shoulder, Oak rises slowly to his feet, doing that thing he does where he makes the rest of the room look tiny.

Red-faced and furious, Edwards stalks to the door and bangs it closed behind him.

'Fucking hell,' breathes Tayls quietly.

The Test

I nod my thanks to Oak. *Now sit down before you fall down, eh, big fella.*

'Take it you're not thinking about making this captaincy thing permanent then, Mac,' Grub chuckles as I walk past him.

I am genuinely furious, but not with the chief exec. *Fucking hell, Jabba!*

I find him in the back room, chair tilted back, staring into space. One look at him and I know what I'm going to do. He looks utterly forlorn.

A fool. A bloody fool. But our *bloody fool.*

'Good morning,' I say from the doorway.

'Is it?' he mutters.

I cross to the kettle, fill it and flick the switch. 'Tea?'

(I'm like the chirpy corporal in an old war film. 'Cuppa tea, sir?'

'Panzer divisions on all sides, no line of retreat and no supplies. D'you think any of that can be helped by a cup of tea?'

'Can't hurt, sir.')

'Go on then,' Jabba growls.

We listen to the kettle boil, then the spoon clinking against the cup. I hand him his tea, he grunts, and I sit down opposite him. The brick-red liquid steams into the silence between us.

'I'll go at the end of the Test,' he says eventually, without taking his eyes from the high window in the corner of the room.

'You know,' I say, 'they woke Churchill one morning with the news that the police had caught one of his cabinet ministers *in flagrante* with a guardsman in Green Park.

'Apparently he said, and I do my best to mimic the old bulldog: "Z'very cold last night," to which the aide replied, "Yes sir. Actually, one of the coldest February nights on record."

'"Good God," Churchill said. "Makes you proud to be British, doesn't it?"'

Jabba nods but doesn't say anything.

'You can ride this out, you know,' I continue. 'You've got enough friends around this place.'

He shakes his head. 'I don't know that I can, actually . . .' He sighs '. . . and I don't want to.' He looks diminished, physically deflated, his heavy body collapsing under its own weight. I don't know what to say.

Eventually I look at my watch and get to my feet. 'I need to pad up.' As I turn to go, he calls me back.

'Mac. Don't fight any more battles for me. This is my fuck-up, not yours.'

For the first time, his eyes come down from the window. I start to object, but he cuts me off. 'Please don't. It just makes it worse.'

When I finally nod agreement, his eyes go back to the window. I go back to the dressing room.

★

The first time I met him was when I was cornered by a journalist in the lobby of a Colombo hotel. I'd arrived from the airport an hour earlier and was on my way to my first England team meeting. The press man had spotted an easy target and come sniffing.

'James isn't going to answer that, and you should know better than to ask it,' the rumbling voice comes from behind me, and I am eclipsed by a large, sweating man in a suit. My mouth, which had hung open for a while, because I couldn't think of a way of closing it that wouldn't get me into trouble, sighs in relief.

'There are only two ways to answer that question, as you well know, both of which land James in shit. Not only *should* you know better, but I know you *do*.'

The journalist directs a pained expression towards Jabba, then tilts his head towards me: 'Have a good evening, James,' he says easily, and wanders away.

My saviour holds out a damp, fleshy mitt. 'Mac, good to meet you at last. Jabba.'

These last two syllables make no immediate sense to me, but I take the hand anyway. He looks at his watch.

'We've got a while until meeting time, shall we grab a drink?'

'Doc! Doc!' The shouting is urgent and coming from the back room.

What now? Surely he hasn't managed to drug himself again?

But I turn round and Tayls is wide awake and strapping his pads on. Then it dawns on me, and with a nameless dread slicing through my guts, I rush into the back room.

He is lying on his side on the floor. Greg is crouched over him, talking calmly but urgently, 'Jabba, can you hear me?'

I turn and scream over my shoulder '*Doc!* We need the doc now!'

I look back down to the body on the floor. His face is grey and twisted out of shape. One eye is open and staring up at me; it seems to focus on me, but I'm not sure. His left arm lies outstretched; the hand flutters like a wounded bird. Other than that, the huge body is still.

The doc pushes past me, kneels by his side. His hands are moving quickly and calmly over the big man. 'Call 999,' he tells Greg. 'Tell them we need an ambulance urgently. Stroke victim, male, fifty-nine years old . . .'

From the dressing room behind me I hear a shout. 'Umps have gone . . .'

270

The Test

Doc looks over his shoulder. 'Go on, Mac. There's nothing you can do here. We'll look after him.'

I realise I'm kneeling down on the floor. I don't remember doing that. I climb to my feet, walk back into the dressing room.

'Mac?' Tayls is standing fully padded and helmeted, ready to go. He is staring at me. I look down; I'm only wearing one pad. 'Mac, we need to go!'

'Yeh. Yeh, just coming,' I say.

Monday 10.58 am

Australia   348 and 405 for 7 dec
England   179 and 231 for 3 (84 overs)

I walk out to bat in a daze.

The members cheer us through the pavilion. The crowd roars us on to the ground, standing and applauding us all the way to the middle. Everything seems to happen remotely, somewhere in the background. I am not there. My mind is still in that small office at the back of the dressing room.

'Mac! Mac!' I realise Tayls is talking to me but I haven't heard him. 'You OK?'

I nod. I look down. My pads are done up wrong. I take off my gloves, reach down and straighten them out.

'Who's on strike?' Tayls asks.

I try to remember yesterday evening but it's just a blur. 'Err . . . you, I think.'

The fielding side break from their huddle and start jogging into position. I try to get my head straight.

Come on, Mac. Switch on here. Jabba's going to be OK. You've got a job to do.

I force myself into the present. There is absolutely nothing I can do for him now. *He's bloody indestructible. He's going to be OK. You just do your job.*

My mind starts to settle down. Switches on to the job at hand. I can do nothing for him except make sure that when he recovers he doesn't discover we lost the Ashes because of him.

The fielders are ready. Tayls settles into his stance.

'Play,' says the umpire.

Through complexity to simplicity.

They say that before you have studied Zen, a mountain is just a mountain.

Then, as you study and gain greater insight, you slowly come to realise that it is more subtle than that. A mountain is no longer just a mountain to you.

When you finally – after years or decades of study – achieve enlightenment, you discover that a mountain . . . is just a mountain.

The path to mastery is the same in many crafts. It is the same for the batsman, the teacher, the coach, or the poet. It is the path from simplicity, through complexity, to simplicity.

The beginner uses simple, basic techniques. He has no choice. They are all he knows and all he can cope with. As he learns and improves, he initially gains greater fluency in these core movements. Then, as he grows more adept, he embraces more and more technical complexity and masters a greater variety of skills and techniques. He studies more deeply the intricacies of his art, and experiments with a wider and wider range of ideas.

But then the process reverses itself. After thousands of hours of immersion in the details and subtleties, and near endless refinements, slowly – over time – he comes to understand what works best for him and what doesn't. The range and complexity of the ideas on which he regularly relies start to shrink.

The apotheosis of this is the master craftsman, for whom true mastery of his art involves a return to simplicity, to a pared-down palette that he now wields to sublime effect. But it is a simplicity born of understanding his true form, and utterly different from the place where he started. Many – most, even – never get there. But the best do.

The very best come to own their game completely. They may still strive every day to improve. They may keep learning right up until the last time they ever pick up a bat. But they own their craft. They own their game.

This is where Tayls is a genius.

As Grub says, he may not have been at the front of the line when they handed out brains, but he must have queued twice for talent.

Neat, compact, easy on the eye, he makes batting look easy. With Rob gone, he is our one genuine world-class player, and he looks in great touch from ball one.

This is his wheelhouse. He was born to play these situations. The greater the pressure, the more there is at stake, the more he stands out. Unhurried and unfazed, he seems to suck the tension out of these moments.

Dumb fuck, hasn't got the imagination to get nervous, Grub says.

The calmness he projects spreads outwards to the rest of the team. I know that up in the pavilion, the dressing room will relax slightly whenever he is on strike.

The ball is still almost new, and their bowlers are tearing in. But we are both playing well.

My body aches all over, and I'm hobbling like an old man between the wickets, but I've found the rhythm I had yesterday and I feel good. I've got time, and I feel I know this pitch now.

The Test

We could do this, you know. We could bloody do this.

Oh you wanker! I shake my head. *Come on, Mac.* I'm angry at myself for that, for starting to think too far ahead.

Back in your box, you numpty. Don't get ahead of yourself.

Peel it back. One ball at a time. *See ball, hit ball.* Get through this over, and then start thinking about the next one.

So which is the real Tayls?

The man in the dressing room – vain, flawed, foolish, if essentially harmless?

Or the once-in-a-generation talent he becomes when he picks up a bat – brilliant, insightful, and utterly nerveless?

I've always wanted to believe that when you see someone do the one thing they love, you are seeing their true form. That watching him bat out here is a window into his soul.

That this is the *real* Tayls.

Not the numpty who thinks the Magna Carta is an ice cream and who can't go a week without losing his phone.

Monday 1.03 p.m.

Australia	348 and 405 for 7 dec
England	179 and 292 for 3 (113 overs)

We make it to lunch.

There are wobbles. We play and miss a few times. Tayls nicks one which doesn't quite carry to the keeper. I have a close LBW shout – the Aussies review the Not Out decision and it stays with the Umpire's Call. But, other than that, we get there without any undue dramas.

When we turn towards the pavilion I realise with a lurch of guilt that I haven't thought about Jabba for well over an hour. As soon as I get back to the room, I drop my kit in my place and head down the corridor to the medical room.

Coming the other way is the chief exec. *Come on then, Mac, time to man up.*

He is about to walk past, head down. I stop him. 'Sorry,' I say, 'about earlier. I was out of order.'

'No,' he says eventually, 'I understand. If I was in trouble, I hope my friends would do the same.' He holds out his hand and I shake it.

'How is he?'

I shake my head and shrug. 'I don't know. I was just going to check now'

The Test

We head into the medical room together. The doc has gone to the hospital, but our physio relays the news. He is stable. They are keeping him sedated for now. They won't know the full extent of the damage until they wake him up, but there is reason to hope that, barring further complications, it won't be too extensive.

'He's not out of the woods, but he's in good hands.'

'Thanks, let me know if you hear anything more.'

Monday 2.35 p.m.

Australia	348 and 405 for 7 dec
England	179 and 322 for 5 (126 overs)
	(56 overs left in the day)

After lunch we are fine for nearly an hour. Then, just before drinks, we lose two wickets in two balls. Tayls gets a leading edge off an innocuous ball from their left-arm spinner and it pops back to the bowler. He stands there in horror as the fielders explode around him. The next man in misses a straight one, first ball, and suddenly the visitors are in full flow again.

They had gone quiet before that. It is hard to sustain energy and belief in the face of a day and a half in the field with no rewards. And even their extraordinary depths of courage and conviction had started to run dry. Over by over you could sense their confidence seeping away into the Lord's turf. With the crowd's incessantly partisan support and enthusiasm echoing around them ball after ball, hour after hour, it must have started to feel like this was not their time or their place. Heavy of limb and weary of mind, they had been visibly flagging.

But not now. Now, they are right back in it. One wicket away from our bowlers. One good hour away from securing the Ashes. Bouncing around with renewed faith and confidence.

And here he comes, the last of our recognised batsmen.

There are good watchers and there are bad watchers, and then there is Grub.

He gets more nervous before the start of his innings than anyone I've ever played with. He is always a wreck walking out to bat, and having the Ashes on a knife-edge, plus a day and a half of waiting with his pads on, has not helped.

As he walks out to the middle he looks grey.

I head over and meet him halfway to the middle.

'Mac?'

'Yes mate?'

'Could you jus' check for uz?'

'What?'

'Are ma arms still attached to ma body? 'Cos they dinna fuckin' feel like it.'

'You're gonna be fine, Grub. It's a piece of piss out here; you'll have no trouble. We've done all the hard work for you; they're all knackered.'

'You say that. But ah reckon that left-arm bastard,' he nods at the quickest of their bowlers, 'is about to try and knock my fuckin' head off. An' am not even allowed to hook him, am ah?'

I can't help it. I'm laughing at him. He's just funny.

'Look, Grub. Me and you are going to bat for a bit. It'll be fun. Maybe we'll lose, maybe we won't. Either way, we're going to have an afternoon we'll never forget. Two days ago we were dead and buried. Now we've got a chance, and we might as well bloody enjoy it. So put a smile on your face and let's keep these buggers under the pump for as long as we can. You never know, we might just save the fucking day.' We punch gloves, and I leave him to take his guard.

He does still look as if he's about to be sick, though.

A thought occurs to me, so I wander back over to him.

'Which pair of socks did you go for in the end?'

He nods cunningly at me and taps the side of his nose, 'Am wearing 'em both, like,' he says quietly.

I glance up at the scoreboard to check the time and see they've got Dad up on the big screen again.

Well, at least he's still here.

For all his skittishness, Grub gets his head down and grafts.

He isn't made for this type of work. He is a cavalier, a dasher; born to play the counterattack, wield the flashing blade. Not for him this infantry slog, the stubborn rearguard.

It's like watching a Ferrari tow a caravan.

But he does it, and does it well enough.

At the next break in play, the twelfth man runs drinks out to us. Grub drops his helmet and gloves and towels the sweat from his head. 'So, Jimmy comes home from school one day,' he grins at me. 'Has to go to his dad and tell him, "Dad, I got suspended again."'

He tells jokes almost constantly, and yet I swear I've almost never heard the same one twice. It's a genuine talent.

'His dad says, "Oh Jimmy! What for this time?"'

Grub pauses to take a swig from his water bottle.

'Jimmy looks sheepish; eventually he says, "I got caught masturbating under the desk."

"'Not again!" His dad shakes his head and says, "You know what, Jimmy? Maybe teaching's just not for you.'"

I laugh. We punch gloves and then go back to our respective ends.

We manage to get to tea without further loss.

I hurry back to the dressing room, but there is no further news on Jabba.

Fifteen years earlier

Climbing a high, grass saddle under a pristine sky, I can see as far as my seventeen-year-old hand or eye can reach or touch; the deceptiveness of distance. Walls like pencil-marks on the far side of the valley are within reach of my outstretched fingers, although we won't get to them for several hours. Then I look back; the hours have flicked me across vast swathes of country, our cottage a mere fleck of brown on the very edge of sight.

I startle a grouse and it hurtles away, skimming the tops of the gorse around us. We labour on under the sun's slow diligence.

Dad loves to hike, and so we are spending half-term in a cottage in the Yorkshire Dales. Today is his most ambitious expedition of the trip: an early rise, a late finish, and thirty miles in between. Mum and Sis have baled on him and, although I wasn't that enthusiastic about the arduous trek, I've been shamed into tagging along.

The rhythm of the day is one I now know well.

This morning, we had woken to an ice-hard silence. Around us dripped sodden trees, their bird-less branches framing a sky scoured clean of clouds.

The Test

At the start of the walk I am impatient, checking my watch regularly to see how long we've been going, amazed to find that it's only fifteen minutes, only twenty-five; God, we've been going for more than half an hour, surely. I parse the first hour, piece by lengthening piece, feeling the miles start to soak themselves into the muscles of my legs.

By the end, I am semi-catatonic; wearily putting one foot in front of the other like a penance. My mind has gone, already showered and slumped by the fire in our cottage, beer in hand, the smells of supper drifting in from the kitchen, the mud hardening on my sodden boots in the corner.

In between, there is the point of stillness, when I stop wondering about how far I've come, how far I have to go, and accept it for what it is. I've been walking for hours, and I've hours still to go. Every ridge will present a view of the next ridge, as every ridge behind me has, the summit still hours and thousands of steps away.

My legs are tired, but strong. My mind, not yet wearied, is freed by the physical monotony, left to soar, high and untroubled.

Heart and thoughts, unpacked by solitude, roam free, even while my feet are harnessed to the path in front. Time stills the cloud-spattered sky above, and I drift beneath it, the mountains rising and falling all around.

Thoughts, nudged into neutral, idle, drift, and eventually come to rest; to a point of gathering stillness, above my moving feet, amidst the turning hills and valleys, below the still and darkening sky.

My feet hurt first. My toes ache from the previous days' walking. My knees and ankles start to grumble as the strain of constant ascent wears at them. My slope-sapped legs and lungs are heavy, but my mind light.

That sense of individual aches and pains is just a part of the first few hours, though.

As the day drags on, and the miles, and the thousands of feet of climbing add up, the aches spread and join up. Until my whole body from my lower back down is just a dull, painful heaviness I can no longer separate out into individual discomforts.

The descents become plods, the ground rising up to hit me at the bottom of each stride.

By late afternoon we are westward enough to see the edge of the Lake District in the distance, where flecks of silver lace the wind-muscled hills.

The sun slides down the sky. Autumn is gathering its slow force around us; the leaves fall, the streams cool.

Behind the hills to the north, winter stalks us, creeping silently down the country's spine to where we clamber over these vast vertebrae pressed through the skin of the landscape.

Monday 5.40 pm

Australia	348 and 405 for 7 dec
England	179 and 386 for 5 (165 overs)
	(17 overs left in the day)

The nearer we get to saving the match, the more nervous I get.

God, I want this.

If I think too much about the people I want this for then it will cripple me. For Beth and the kids watching at home on TV. For Mum. For every friend who reached out with text or phone call when the press came after me. For Dad. For Stocksy, who got me all the way to the England team, and then got me back in again after I cocked it up the first time. For Jabba, lying alone in a hospital room.

But, most of all, I want it for the other blokes up there in the room. For the players who for years now have stood next to me in victory, and stood by me in defeat, who've carried me when I've failed, and cheered me when I've succeeded, who've followed me into this match and done everything I asked, and risked their bodies and careers to try and get us over the line.

I want each of them to wake up tomorrow with that background glow of pleasure, and walk into their homes

287

with their heads up, and smiles on their faces when they see their families again.

I want that.

I want it so much that it is close to agony.

And then, suddenly, when we are within touching distance of making it to safety, it all starts to unravel.

Grub fends a short ball to gulley. The touring team celebrates like they've won the World Cup. They know they've opened up an end to attack our tail, and that a match that had almost slipped from their grasp is very much back up for grabs.

And now we are falling. Each new batsman's stay is briefer than the last. We are slipping, sliding, accelerating towards the abyss of defeat. Composure gone, panic setting in, running out of wickets . . .

. . . when, finally, like a falling climber's last desperate swing of his axe biting into the snow, halting his slide and holding his weight, we manage to break the momentum of our fall.

9 wickets down
(5 overs left in the day)

I stand waiting. From high on the stands, the flags wave their shadows at my feet, lazily stroking the turf, sublimely unconcerned.

I can't believe it's come down to this.

Oak limps out to the middle, his bat hanging like a twig from one large hand. I hobble over to meet him.

'Mac.'

'Oak.'

I look down at his knee, then at mine. 'No quick singles then.' He half smiles in response and shakes his head, then shuffles onwards to the striker's end to take guard.

The floodlights are on, have been for half an hour now, but the conditions aren't going to save us. The sun has come out, low in the sky to the West.

Thirty balls.

Thirty balls.

Why did I do it?

Whatever the reasons are, they are not the stories my mind tells me later.

Memories are no help in discerning the truth. They are shadows on a cave wall, post-hoc rationalisations.

Where is a decision *actually* made?

The mystery is starkest when I bat. The part of me that thinks and experiences is too slow to hit a ball. By the time I know the bowler has bowled the ball, it is already passing me. So something else takes over: instinct, training, hard-wired reflexes, fast but thoughtless.

Why did I do *that*? I often wondered, after a poor shot, or another failed attempt to get sober. There are hidden operators somewhere that make the decision, and then inform *me – the conscious me –* of what they have decided, at which point I come up with the rationalisations to fit it.

The truth is, though, that I found myself doing something and tracked backwards until I found a reason. Not *the* reason, just *a* reason.

Where is the ghost that makes the decisions? The ball flashes towards me, my hands are there, my feet and weight have moved, my body has shaped itself for the shot.

Not always perfectly. Not always matching the image of the ideal I have in my head.

But fast. Impossibly fast.

My brain runs my body. Beats my heart, breathes my lungs, stiffens my muscles so I don't fall over. My conscious mind runs behind time, telling itself the story as it goes.

Towards the end, when I drank, I didn't want to. It rarely made any sense to. But I did it. And the decision to do it arrived ready-made, a *fait accompli*. Something took over and I found out what I'd decided afterwards.

Just like my cover drive.

Thirty balls.

There are moments in any match when all is focused into a consequence of seconds; when every potential storyline collapses into the singularity of a ball's collision with the turf. And let us not forget, that God (as Einstein should have said), plays dice like an addict down to his last blind. Whatever, whenever, and whoever we are, we can only survive in the aggregate. We can only find meaning in the long run.

Reality, Amos Tversky says, *is not a point. It is a cloud of possibility.*

Thirty balls.

Thirty balls between triumph and despair.

I'm on strike. I play out the first four balls. Try to work a single off the fifth, but play and miss. The last ball is a high bouncer, I start to take it on but pull out. *Too risky, going to have to trust the big man.*

Twenty-four balls to go.

Oak does OK. It's not a great over, to be honest. The bowler tries too hard, and wastes half of his six balls. One play-and-miss, otherwise no drama.

Eighteen balls to go.

I can bat this end and face twelve, leave Oak the other six, or I can try and nick a single towards the end of the over. Do that twice and he might only need to face two or three.

The bowler gets to the crease and bowls. *Shit*, my mind is nowhere, still playing with the permutations of strike. The ball hammers into the pitch just outside off-stump. I leave it, have to; I'm flat-footed, in no position to play it. To my horror it snakes back up the slope towards the stumps. I wait for the death rattle, but it doesn't come, just gasps and exasperated curses from the slips. The bowler stands in the middle of the wicket, hands on his head, staring in disbelief. He'd gone up in celebration as he watched the ball hurtle into the wicket.

The replay up on the screen shows just how close the ball was: a millimetre or two at most.

Ah well, there are two types of leave . . .

Maybe remember to think about your batting, eh Mac?

Seventeen balls to go.

The ground is buzzing as the big screen replays the clip. The fate of the Ashes being decided by how many coats of varnish they put on my off-stump.

I walk a few steps away from the pitch, lift my head and gaze at the sky. Mountains are dressed as clouds, and lit by the evening sun, supremely untroubled by the outcome of the next few balls. The sky is calm, and after a few seconds so am I. I go back to the crease.

The next two balls hit the middle of my bat.

There is then a lengthy discussion among the fielding team. Keeper and captain jog the length of the pitch to talk to the bowler. After much pointing and back and forth, the field is adjusted, everyone goes back to their marks, and the bowler runs in again. The ball flies harmlessly down the leg-side; the bowler curses himself and kicks the turf bitterly.

Fourteen balls to go.

Now they have a dilemma. They can bounce two over my head, to keep Oak on strike for the start of the next over, backing themselves to get him out given a full six balls at him. But, with only fourteen balls left in the match, it is tough to waste two of them by doing that.

So now there is another meeting of their Brains Trust. This over is taking forever. I go back to the clouds. Still calm, still oblivious. And, whatever happens, they will still be there tomorrow. To the West, a shaft of sunlight flares through a gap in the clouds like an expensive stage-show effect.

The bowler is ready. I go back to the crease. Both balls are bounced high over my head. I still haven't worked out the permutations to my satisfaction, but it doesn't matter, I can't safely take either ball on anyway, so I watch them sail past, then limp down the wicket to talk to Oak.

Twelve balls to go.

Oak is on strike.

Twelve balls to go.

The first ball is dug in short, angled into his ribs. He manages to fend it away safely, and it rolls off towards the vacant fine-leg area. Perfect, we can jog through for a single and I can see off the rest of the over. This bowler is definitely the greater threat at the moment.

I trot down the wicket; even with my knee this is the easiest of singles, the fielder hasn't even reached the ball yet. Then I look up, and see Oak hasn't moved. He is just standing in his ground watching the fielder jog to the ball. But now the excited shouts from the Australians cause him to look round. Our eyes meet in horror. I am over halfway down the pitch, nearer to his end than mine. I slam on the brakes, just as he sets off, then for an abject second we do a sort of unco-ordinated dance: shall we, shan't we? Too late.

'*No! Get back!*' I hear myself shouting the words and I'm turning to sprint back to my end. But, my first step slips under me and I go down in the middle of the pitch . . . *Fuck, fuck, fuck* . . . and I'm scrambling, trying desperately to get my feet under me, lurching towards the crease like a panicked drunk. I don't look back; the bowler in front of me is by the stumps, screaming for the ball. I am five yards short . . . three yards . . . I throw myself at the line . . . the ball arrives as I hit the ground.

I look at the turf three inches in front of my face. *Seriously, Mac, what the fuck is going on here?*

I haul myself upright, wave an apology to Oak. He lifts his hand in acknowledgement.

Right then, no singles it is.

Eleven balls to go.

The next ball is just outside off-stump; Oak fences at it and misses. The fielders go up in a half-hearted appeal, but he clearly hasn't touched it. Now I'm nervous. Now that we haven't taken the single, every ball feels lethal. I should be at that end. I should be on strike.

I look up. The clouds have barely moved. They don't care whether he misses it or nicks it. Don't care now, and won't tomorrow.

The third ball of the over is a beauty; it angles in towards the stumps, then just holds its line as it pitches. Oak pushes at it, flat-footed, the ball flies through to the keeper who takes it and hurls it into the air in triumph. Every Australian in the ground is up, roaring at the umpire. My heart drops through the floor; there was definitely a clear noise as the ball passed the bat. I look to the umpire; for an age he doesn't move, and then slowly shakes his head, Not Out.

I look to their captain. Without any hesitation he makes the sign to review the decision. The Australians surround the bowler and high-five. *They've won, they know it.*

I walk down to a grim-faced Oak.

'Did you hit it?'

He looks uncertain. 'Not sure. There was a sound, but I didn't feel anything.' He shrugs.

We turn to look at the big screen.

The first replay is inconclusive. The second shows the hint of a gap between bat and ball. I look over to the Aussies, where the celebrations have paused. They are frowning up at the screen. Hot Spot doesn't show anything where the ball has passed the edge, but there is a mark on the tip of the back pad. Further replays confirm it, the bat has missed the ball, but flicked the very top of Oak's back pad, hence the noise.

The umpire confirms his Not Out decision, and we all go back to our positions. The whole ground is roaring. Half the crowd are on their feet, applauding Oak's survival.

God, this is painful.

Nine balls to go.

The next ball is short again. Oak keeps his hands low, grits his teeth and lets the ball cannon into his shoulder. Short leg catches it, tosses it back to the bowler, and he marches back to his mark.

The penultimate ball of the over nips back and hits him on the pad; there is half an appeal, but it has clearly done too much and is missing the stumps.

Last ball of the over. One more ball for Oak to survive and then it's all down to me.

The bowler charges in; this is his last chance, the last thing he will do in the series. He hurls the ball down, but the big fella is equal to it. The ball hits the middle of the bat and rolls back up the pitch. The crowd roars its approval, and now the whole ground are on their feet to applaud our number eleven's survival.

I walk down and punch gloves.

'Well done, mate. Good job. You can go and put your feet up now.'

Six balls to go.

I'm on strike. Every fielder is in a catching position now. They are chirping away under helmets on either side in front of me, and there is a complete umbrella of slips behind.

Six balls to go.

The first one is dug in short. I see it early, duck under it. It sails harmlessly into the keeper's gloves.

Five balls to go.

The next one is a very good ball. Quick, full, reversing back into middle and leg. I am just quick enough, manage to jab the bat down on it, and it squirts out into the leg-side.

Four to go.

Another good ball, probing at the stumps. Again, I'm equal to it. It hits the middle of the bat. I take a deep breath. *Switch off.* Wander away towards square leg, and then come back to the crease again. *Switch back on.*

Three balls to go.

This one is short and straight, I go back and up on to my toes, determined to get on top of it and drop it short of the close catchers around me. But it doesn't bounce; instead it shoots through low, and thuds into my boot, right in front of the stumps. At the end of two full days, the pitch has finally betrayed me.

After all that, I never had a chance.

The umpire's finger swings up straight away. The bowler drops to the ground in the middle of the pitch, arms aloft. His teammates engulf him, bouncing up and down in their triumph.

The Test

I find myself on my knees, staring down the wicket at the point where the ball pitched, unable to believe that it has all come down to this.

'Mac.'

I look up and next to me is the Aussie captain. He holds out his hand, I take it, and he helps me up.

He puts his other hand on my shoulder and shakes his head slowly. 'Well batted, mate. Hell of a knock. Hell of a knock.'

'Thanks,' I say, and then am just about able to get the words out. 'Congratulations, well played.'

He shrugs, lost for words.

We turn together, walk off towards the pavilion. Now that it's over I'm like a puppet with its strings cut. I am barely able to put one foot in front of the other. Steve puts his arm round my shoulders – giving the papers their back-page photo for tomorrow in the process – part comfort, part support. He chuckles.

'You know what the Aussies say,' he grins finally. '*It's a shit game . . .*'

'*. . . played by pricks,*' we finish together. I manage a smile in response.

'It always was.'

And then we are in the middle of the two teams and the support staff for the end-of-series handshakes.

'Well played,' I say each time I shake a hand.

'Well done, well played.'

'Well done . . .'

At the end of the line is our chief selector. He shakes my hand, 'Bad luck, Mac. Unbelievable knock, really well played.'

'Thanks, Tony.'

'Let's get that knee patched up ready for the winter tours, eh?' He thinks he's being reassuring, letting me know my place is no longer under threat.

I think we're past that, aren't we?

I smile, thank him again, and head up the pavilion steps. I'm concentrating so hard on not collapsing that it takes me a moment to realise that the members are standing and applauding, and an echoing roar is coming from around the ground. I look round and I'm on the big screen. The whole ground is standing, and both teams have stopped at the bottom of the steps to applaud me off. *Well, that's a moment.* I lift my bat to acknowledge the applause. There is an answering roar from the stands.

Yes, that is a moment.

Dad is up on the big screen again. *Jeez, he's getting some airtime, isn't he?*

I lift my bat towards him. Then turn and go into the pavilion.

Monday, 7.25 p.m.

The phone rings, I hear her pick up and start to answer, but then the line breaks up,

'Beth . . . Beth . . . ? Can you hear me? Beth . . . I can't . . . I can't hear you.' The line is dead.

I redial, but just get her voicemail.

'This is Beth. Leave a message and I'll get back to you.'

'Turn the news on, Beth. I want . . .' but my voice is in danger of betraying me and I have to stop. I try again. 'Beth . . . I want to come home . . .'

I make two more calls, to Dad and to Stocksy. I would ask their opinion, but the decision is already made. That they both already know what I'm phoning to say is tacit agreement anyway.

I walk into the press conference and sit down. The microphones crouch in front of me, ready to strike. I clear my throat, and start to read from the sheet of paper in front of me. Nothing comes out but a croak. Automatically my eyes go to the corner where Jabba is, but find only an empty chair.

I take a sip of water, close my eyes, take a breath.

Open them again.

'I would like to announce my retirement from all forms of cricket . . .'

*

A couple of hours later, all the presentations and media interviews are finished, the TV cameras have been turned off, and the crowds are gone. In the twilight, a platoon of workers are slowly plucking the stands clean of the day's rubbish.

Both sets of players and coaches have crammed themselves into our dressing room, to share a beer and spend an hour or so making a pretence of normalising relations after three months of open hostility.

I am standing in a small circle of Aussie players, nodding, smiling and trying to listen to a story I've already lost track of. My phone buzzes in my pocket. Grateful for the interruption, I glance at the caller ID and, seeing who it is, slip out on to the empty balcony to take the call.

'Hey, you.'

'Hey, Mac.'

I sink on to the bench and close my eyes, wrap myself in her voice.

'So, anyway, I saw on the news you quit your job.'

'Yeah, I did do that.'

'Now we're both unemployed then.'

'Kinda looks that way for the moment. Any thoughts?'

'I hear they need bar staff in The Royal Oak.'

'Working in a pub? There might be one or two reasons why that's not a good fit for me.'

'Well, I didn't mean for *you*.' I am enjoying listening to the smile in her voice. It's been a while.

But when she continues, she is quieter, sombre. 'I'm sorry, Mac, about the match, I mean. I . . .' She tails off.

'I know. Shit way to end a long day.'

There is a pause.

I take a deep breath. 'So, anyway, while I've got you . . . I was wondering what your plans were for the next thirty to fifty years?'

'Well . . .' I can still hear the smile, and the arch of the eyebrow. '. . . I don't think I've got much inked in at this stage. Why? What have you got in mind?'

We have a strong tendency towards determinism when we try to understand sport. Something happened, therefore that was the way it was always going to happen. With the benefit of hindsight, the result appears, as Mike Brearley puts it, 'not only inevitable, but morally appropriate'.

So we get sucked into trying to determine the root causes of what happened with the assumption that this will make us better able to predict the immediate future.

It is akin to autopsying a corpse to find the cause of death, and then using that as your diagnosis for the next patient to walk through the door.

Sport is mostly random variation, far more noise than signal. In the language of maths, it is not deterministic, but chaotic. *Chaos: When the present determines the future, but the approximate present does not approximately determine the future.*

To accurately assess past outcomes we must retreat behind the veil of ignorance. Be aware of all the potential paths a match could have taken, but ignorant of the one that it actually did. That something happened does not mean it was bound to happen.

And yet still some defeats are *so* shocking, *so* comprehensive, that we cannot resist seeing in them an almost moral judgement on the losing side's frailties and the victorious side's superiority of method, strategy and philosophy.

But I've been in this game a while now, and we were never as smart as they said we were. Nor were we ever as stupid or inept as they said.

We are closer to the roulette wheel than we care to imagine. Most of our stories are the erroneous hindsight of our pattern-spotting brains when faced with what are, largely, random events.

For all its complexity and nuance, there is often a brutal, mathematical simplicity to sport. However much we might talk about styles of play, mental strength or fallibility. For all the thought given to the endlessly layered, interlocking details of technique and tactics, you can still predict a batsman's probability of getting a hundred to within a few tenths of a percentage point, knowing nothing but his average.

Each time you walk to the crease, you roll the dice. Sometimes they fall your way. Sometimes they don't. The long view is sane, and ordered, but the present is chaotic.

And so, into the threshing machine of this randomness marches the player, heartbreakingly invested in the outcome.

It isn't life and death, and it isn't, as Bill Shankly would have it, more serious than that. But it does matter. It has to matter. The moment it doesn't, it loses the magic that holds the whole endeavour together. And for us, it is a career, a future, our hopes and dreams, in which, on any given day, we are the playthings of blind, arrogant chance.

And nor can you walk out there believing your efforts don't matter, that the result is random, and the chips will fall as they may. Because the moment you try less than your best, you fail. You have to invest full faith in your efforts. That this dichotomy is beyond almost all of us, is at the heart of our courage.

Handling the random variation, the luck, the unfairness, the beguiling periods of success, the player, walled off from the nuanced view of the observer, can see only triumph and tragedy, and so is buffeted on the winds of fortune.

That we get up each morning and go on regardless is the soul of the drama, and the peculiar heroism of it. It isn't bravery unless you are afraid.

That we continue to sail, regardless, into the heart of the storm that we can't understand, again and again, is what makes us admirable.

Is what makes us worth watching.

EPILOGUE

The end of the summer

My phone rings as I am swinging the car into the drive. I pull up, listen to it ring over the speakers and let it go to voicemail. A few moments later, a text message pops up on the screen with a ping, '*Hi Mac, you don't know me. Tayls gave me your number. I'd really like to speak to you about a business opportunity that you might . . .*' I click the phone off and lean back in my seat. I take a deep breath and try to still the butterflies fluttering around in my guts.

The front garden is less overgrown than it should be. It looks as if someone has been popping in to keep it in check. And, if I had to guess, I'd say that that someone lives in the next village and teaches English. *Better take him something nice next time I go round.*

Gingerly I prise myself out of the car, dig the front door keys out of my pocket and walk slowly up the path. I'm moving carefully, like a convalescent, wary of the raw feeling sloshing around my chest.

Easy, Mac. This is going to be OK.

My chest is tight, my breath coming fast and short.

The drift of mail behind the front door makes it hard to

open, but I manage to shoulder my way in. Slowly, I move from room to room, just letting myself get used to being back.

'*I'm going to need time, Mac.*' That was the last thing she said to me, '*Let's just take things slowly, OK?*'

A couple of hours later I am halfway down the list of jobs I've scribbled out for the afternoon when I hear a second car pull into the driveway and park up behind mine. I walk to the open front door of the house and grin.

They both see me at the same time.

'Daddy!'